THE ANIMAL INSIDE

OTHER TITLES FROM BLACK BEACON BOOKS

Novels by Cameron Trost:

Dead on the Dolmen
Flicker
Letterbox
The Tunnel Runner

Collections by Cameron Trost:

Oscar Tremont, Investigator of the Strange and Inexplicable
The Animal Inside
Hoffman's Creeper and Other Disturbing Tales

Anthologies:

Samhain Screams
The Black Beacon Books of Mystery
The Black Beacon Book of Ghosts
The Black Beacon Book of Horror
The Black Beacon Book of Pirates
Steampunk Sleuths
Tales from the Ruins
A Hint of Hitchcock
Murder and Machinery
Shelter from the Storm
Lighthouses
Subtropical Suspense

blackbeaconbooks.com

THE ANIMAL INSIDE

A Collection of Strange Tales
by Cameron Trost

**BLACK
BEACON
BOOKS**

Black Beacon Books
www.blackbeaconbooks.com

ISBN: 9780992321178

To my sons, Fergus and Lucien.
I hope these tales will entertain you one day and give you pause
to reflect on what it means to be a good man. You've both made
me want to be a better person, more than you'll ever know.

Cameron Trost is an author of mystery, suspense, horror, and post-apocalyptic fiction best known for his puzzles featuring Oscar Tremont, Investigator of the Strange and Inexplicable. He has written four novels, "Dead on the Dolmen", "Flicker", "Letterbox", and "The Tunnel Runner", and three collections, "Oscar Tremont, Investigator of the Strange and Inexplicable", "Hoffman's Creeper and Other Disturbing Tales", and "The Animal Inside". He runs the independent press, Black Beacon Books, and is a member of the Australian Crime Writers Association and The Short Mystery Fiction Society. Originally from Brisbane, Australia, Cameron lives with his wife and two sons near Guérande in southern Brittany, between the rugged coast and treacherous marshland.

www.camerontrost.com

The Animal Inside is a collection of thirteen strange and twisted stories that will take you for a walk along the fine line between insanity and reason, the peculiar and the prosaic, and the animal kingdom and human society, then leave you wondering where one ends and the other begins. These tales will confuse, amuse, shock, and intrigue, but they will also cause you to contemplate your very own animal inside.

CLEOPATRA'S MYSTERY BOX

'Put your hand inside my box and tell me what you feel.'

It was the first time Cleopatra had invited Andrew back to her house. Her father was out west on a field trip, tracking desert lizards, and her mother and younger sister were down the coast for the weekend. They were sitting on her bed, he cross-legged at the foot, and she nestled at the head in a cloud of velvet and patchwork cushions. Her Egyptian eyes watched him intently, and her porcelain face was so stern it simply had to be fighting back a smile.

'Is this foreplay?' he asked, hoping to make her crack.

She pursed her purple lips.

'It's a game,' she said eventually.

'What kind of game?'

'My game.'

'So, you've played it before?'

'Well, it wouldn't be my game if I hadn't, would it?' She frowned. 'You can ask pointless questions or you can play. It's up to you.'

'I want to play.'

'Just put your hand inside and tell me what you feel. If you guess correctly, you can ask me to do something for you.'

He stared into her dark brown eyes, full of childish mischief and timeless mystery, then dropped his gaze to the box in her hands. The object didn't look out of place in her boudoir, which reminded him of a private museum he'd recently visited in Dublin, the city his parents called home. Even so, the box hypnotised him, clamped between fingers adorned with pewter owls, serpents, and deer staring at him over white knuckles and liquorice nails. It was polished oak with silver corner protectors and hinges. On the side facing Andrew, a sliding panel with a latch was open, and there were two rectangular pieces of red velvet acting as curtains.

'I can ask you to do whatever I like if I guess what it is?' Andrew checked, his eyes still fixed on the box.

'That's right. If you can tell me exactly what's inside. Of course, I may not invite you to play again if your request reveals a side of you that I find too ugly.'

He moved closer, slowly reaching out, and as his hand parted the soft curtains, he raised his gaze to meet hers.

Neither of them uttered a word.

His fingers fell upon the small object. It was hard and oddly shaped, with five sides culminating in a point at one end and a multifaceted domelike contour at the other. It reminded him of a pyramid, albeit an imperfect one. It had to be a gemstone of some kind.

He was about to tell her that he knew what it was when he felt something attached to it at the domelike end. He rubbed it between his fingers and realised that it was a chain with fine links.

Cleopatra detected a faint smile on his lips. 'You think you know?'

'I think so,' he admitted. 'Give me a moment to think about it.'

'Take your time,' she whispered teasingly. Her sweet-scented breath aroused him; a seduction of honey, lemon, and mint.

He closed his eyes and continued exploring the object with his fingers, knowing that Cleopatra was confident he would get it wrong. He'd seen it in her eyes and read it on her lips, despite her best efforts to remain indecipherable. She wanted him to beat her, to prove that he was worthy. He'd never made love to her in her bed, where she'd be more comfortable and uninhibited than anywhere else. It would be on her terms, but she was offering him the chance to sate his hunger too.

He'd been thinking of an earring, but now ruled that possibility out because his fingers had noticed that the chain was too long and without a hook at the end. It couldn't be a pendant either as it didn't form a loop. A gemstone on a chain that wasn't meant to be worn. He could describe the object, but Cleopatra wanted him to tell her precisely what it was. The problem was that the only thing Andrew could think of that might hang from a single length of chain was a bath plug.

He opened his eyes and registered Cleopatra's admiration before she could react, setting her face into a stern mask again. Right or wrong, she would adore him.

They sat like statues for several seconds, and Andrew started to feel as though she were hypnotising him. That impression allowed the most probable solution to dawn on him.

A knowing grin appeared on his face.

'Oh, really?' she said. 'Go on, take a stab.'

He drew a deep breath through his nostrils, keeping his lips sealed, and spoke a single word. 'Pendulum.'

The look came back like a bolt of lightning. The porcelain didn't crack, it melted, and the eyes of the seductress opened up to let him in, allowing him to fill her.

'What do you want me to do?'

He told her, explaining that he wanted them to be truly together this time, reassuring her that once, just once, wouldn't pose a risk. She didn't like it but had no choice. He'd played her game and won, and more importantly than that, she loved him, heart and soul.

From that day forth, whenever they were alone together, they played the game. Sometimes, Andrew guessed correctly, but Cleopatra made it more difficult every time. After several weeks, her disposition began to change. Andrew couldn't work out why, nor could he quite put his finger on just how she was changing. The façade he'd become accustomed to – that had, perhaps, first caught his attention – was crumbling away. It was clear that she was aware of this metamorphosis. She was happier than ever, but also a little frightened. Andrew assumed it was a normal development in their relationship. He'd been with her longer than with any of his ex-girlfriends, and he knew it was the same for Cleopatra. She was in love with him, that he knew, and he supposed he was in love with her too.

'I have to tell you something,' she announced after sex one evening, pulling her black leggings up over her milky skin like a lunar eclipse.

It was only the second time they had made love at her place. Andrew had identified the hibiscus flower in her mystery box and requested the site of their lovemaking. Ever since she'd told him about her father's reptile room, he'd wanted to do her there. He'd imagined that fornicating in the middle of a room walled with vivariums full of lizards and snakes with phallic bodies and flickering tongues would be highly arousing, and indeed it had been.

'What is it?' he prompted her while he tied a knot in the condom.

'There was no need for you to wear that,' she said, her eyes questioning.

'I don't understand.'

'The condom,' she said. 'There was no point.'

His eyes widened instantly, his face suddenly reptilian.

'I wasn't sure until today. I took a test. The first time we played the game, when you asked me to let you come inside me, and you thought there was no risk if we only did that once. Well, you were wrong.'

She was smiling at him, her eyes full of boundless love. Never before had she been so vulnerable, so childlike and yet so womanly at the same time.

'Say something, my love. Aren't you happy?'

'Happy?' he growled. 'You expect me to be happy? Are you insane?'

Cleopatra opened her mouth, but no words escaped her lips of smeared lavender.

'How could you do this to me?' Andrew hissed.

She shook her head, and it looked as though she would faint. Her eyes were swimming.

'I didn't *do* this. It was your request.'

Andrew took a deep breath and then blew the air back out through tense lips. He still held the used condom pathetically between finger and thumb. His penis was now limp.

'We'll work it out,' Cleopatra reassured him. 'We're not ready, I know, but we'll be fine, the three of us.'

'The three of us?' He scowled. 'You're not serious, are you?'

She burst into tears.

'You're going to have an abortion,' he told her as evenly as he could.

'I love you.'

'It was a stupid mistake. We won't make it again. You'll have an abortion and we'll forget all about it.'

'I won't kill our child,' she snapped, wiping the tears from her eyes, smudging her black makeup.

'We can't have a child together. I'm not ready. You can't do this to me.'

'I didn't do this to you. *You* did this. I thought you'd be happy.'

He got to his feet and pulled his trousers up. 'I can't deal with you just now. You're acting all crazy. Call me once you've sorted it out.'

'You're leaving? You're walking out on me?'

Without a word, he rushed out of the reptile room.

It wasn't until Friday afternoon that Cleopatra finally succeeded in catching up with Andrew. She skipped her last lecture of the week and parked her old Magna a little further down the street from his house, under the shade of a Moreton Bay fig tree, knowing he'd arrive on foot from the nearest bus stop.

When she saw him, she got out of the car and closed the door as quietly as possible. He was wearing a black hat with a wide brim and was looking at the pavement, so he didn't notice Cleopatra until they had both reached the gate. He raised his head, and the look Cleopatra saw on his face made her take a step back.

'Andrew, listen to me,' she begged. 'Please.'

'There's nothing to talk about. It's over between us.'

'Andrew, I love you,' she said slowly. 'I love you, and you love me.'

He stared over her head, not daring to maintain eye contact. 'No, I don't.'

15

Cleopatra wanted to tell him that he was a heartless monster, a selfish pig, incapable of accepting responsibility for his own acts. Now, when his burgeoning family needed him most, he was so ready to abandon them without a second thought. The urge to throw all that at him was so very strong. Her right hand was itching to slap him and her tongue was swimming in saliva, ready to be spat all over his impassive face, but she resisted the temptation. His love had proven so fickle and his behaviour had changed so quickly. She no longer knew him at all. There was so much hate in his icy regard that she feared his reaction to any sign of physical aggression. The evening news was full of reports of women murdered by men they thought loved them. If that happened to her, it would mean the death of the human being blossoming inside her.

'It's over. Don't come near me again,' he said, his voice void of even the slightest hint of guilt or regret.

She bit her tongue and pressed her hands against her thighs.

He turned to open the garden gate.

'Wait, Andrew,' she pleaded. 'What if we play my game?'

'It's too late for games,' he replied without turning around, shaking his head as though talking to a silly child. His hand was on the gate, ready to push it open.

'If you guess correctly, I'll do whatever you want.'

Andrew turned around and looked her in the eye. 'Whatever I want?'

She closed her eyes. 'Yes,' she whispered.

'If I guess correctly and you do what I want, you will hate me for it. What would be the point of that?'

'I could never hate you for winning the game. I created it and nothing means more to me. Whatever happens, I will accept the result.'

'If I don't guess correctly, what happens?'

'You know the rules, Andrew. There's no obligation on either of us if you lose.'

'If this is the only way I can stop you from making the biggest mistake of your life, I'm willing to give it a go.'

Cleopatra breathed a sigh of relief.

'Do you have the box?'

'It's in the car. I wanted to go back to where we first made love, but I'm not so sure now.'

'Why aren't you sure?'

A flicker of doubt crossed her face.

'You know I would never do anything to hurt you, Cleopatra. Whatever the outcome, I won't lay a finger on you. You know that, don't you?'

'Yes, I know,' she lied.

'Well, let's do it,' he said. 'Where are you parked?'

Cleopatra led the way. She could feel Andrew's eyes sizing her up as they walked in silence, and she told herself she'd never understand, not in a million years, how anybody's love could falter so easily.

They didn't speak a word to each other as the suburban queen drove her rusty chariot back to where they had first made love. For a quarter of an hour, she kept her hands on the wheel and her eyes on the winding road that took them into the forest. Her rings glinted every few seconds as they drove through patches of sunlight, then the forest grew denser as they approached their destination.

She parked at the entrance to the track and glanced at Andrew as she removed the key from the ignition. She caught a glimpse of the smile on his face, just before it disappeared. Their first time had been here, on New Year's Eve; just the two of them, away from the city crowds. They had read poetry to each other by candlelight and drunk copiously. The sounds and smells of the forest had swallowed them, making them part of the magical realm. Without watches or smart phones, time had stood still until the distant popping of fireworks announced the midnight hour.

Now, they were back again, this time, their love in ruins. There was only the faintest glimmer of hope, fainter than a firefly's glow.

Andrew opened the door and got out, eager to get on with it, not wanting to let Cleopatra see that the memories of this place held sway.

She got out, removed the box from the boot of the car, and followed him down the meandering track. It led them into a gully, weaving its way around giant trees with tangled roots and past boulders that had witnessed aeons. At the end, they recognised the spot where it had all begun. They had passed the evening on a flat rock overhanging the creek, which had been trickling at the time but was now bone dry. It had felt quite soft at the time, together on the rock with nothing but an old picnic blanket to lie on. Alcohol and arousal had distracted them from their discomfort.

The gully hadn't changed at all since that night, and Andrew supposed that was why she'd begged him to return there with her.

He stopped on the very spot where they had been and turned to her. She was so strangely beautiful with her Egyptian eyes and her mystery box. He knew he had to guess correctly. She would do what they both knew had to be done, and he would forgive her. In no time, the whole sorry episode would become a vague memory.

'It was the most marvellous night of my life.'

'For me too,' he admitted. 'I'll never forget it.'

'We can relive it, you know? We could come back here as a family. Wouldn't that be just the most glorious thing in the world?'

He groaned. 'I don't know what's wrong with you. You can't accept that we made a mistake and need to deal with it. You have to get rid of it. Then, we can put this behind us, and one day, when the time is right, maybe we can have a baby.'

She looked down at the box. 'Either way, you win. If you guess correctly, I have to fulfil your request. If you're wrong, you'll abandon us.'

He made no reply.

'Is that how it's to be?'

'It was your idea. It's what you wanted,' he reminded her.

'I understand,' she said bitterly, reluctantly holding the box out.

He took a step closer and reached inside. They stared into each other's eyes, and Cleopatra started to cry.

'What do we have?' Andrew wondered as his hand explored, but no sooner had he uttered those words than a look of pure terror distorted his face.

'A snake?' he hissed through trembling lips.

He acted instinctively, jerking his hand out of the box, but wasn't fast enough. The snake struck three times in lightning succession, sinking its fangs into his flesh.

Cleopatra quickly slid the panel across the red curtains and closed the latch.

Andrew looked at his hand and found six puncture marks.

'You psychotic bitch! Is it venomous?' he roared at Cleopatra.

'Highly,' she replied. 'Almost as venomous as your unfeeling black heart, you pig! I gave you my body, my heart, and my soul. I invited you to play my game, and you got me pregnant. It was your request, not mine. Then, after all that, in the blink of an eye, you asked me to end the life you made in me. You're so willing to deny your own child! Well, if you won't live with us, you won't live at all. That's an inland taipan in the box. It bit you three times, so you'll probably be dead in less than half an hour.'

'You have to do something for me though. That's the rule, bitch!' he growled, his fury overriding his fear.

Cleopatra hesitated, thinking about the new life inside her.

'Yes,' she admitted. 'I can't break my own rules.'

He felt his pockets for his smart phone, but couldn't find it.

'Shit!' he yelled.

'Do you want me to tell you where it is? Is that your final request?'

He glared at her, torn between a hunger for revenge and the will to live, knowing that he couldn't have both.

'You're running out of time, Andrew. What do you want me to do?'

'You evil witch! I wish I'd never met you!'

She shook her head in disgust. 'The feeling is mutual, but it's too late for that. The venom is working its way through your body. Do you have a final request?'

He had no choice. 'I want you to call for help,' he begged.

She knelt down and placed the box on the ground, then, imitating the snake, sprang up and pushed Andrew with all her might. He stumbled backwards and fell to the creek bed, hitting the ground with a thud.

'Help!' she called softly into the forest.

With that, she wiped her eyes dry, seized the box, and headed back to the car.

THE CHURCH OF ASAG

Isisford was just what the Inglewood family had expected, a hick-infested hell-hole in the middle of nowhere. Gary had tried to remain optimistic, thinking of it as a close-knit country town a stone's throw from Longreach, but the stunned look on his face bore witness to his disappointment.

The overpacked station wagon rolled warily along the main street. The Inglewoods had tried to bring all their earthly possessions with them, but even a spacious car like theirs had its limits.

They passed an art gallery, and its recycled rubbish sculptures with beer caps for eyes seemed to watch the family from behind a dirty display window.

Further along, outside the news agency, a haggard farmer observed them as he puffed away at a cigarette.

The station wagon kept rolling along.

Two women were about to enter an old worker's cottage that served as the post office when they stopped in their tracks and turned around.

The senior of the pair spoke to her junior, who then stared at the car. She seemed to be trying to see who was inside the moving vehicle. She smiled and seemed to sigh in relief.

The station wagon stopped in the middle of the road while Gary and Amanda tried to work out which street to take. That was possibly the only advantage of living in a backwater like Isisford; you could sit in the middle of the street and play a game of chess or two without bothering traffic.

'This is the one, honey,' Greg Inglewood reassured his wife. He turned off the main street and into a dead end that held four houses on each side before the bitumen dropped and crumbled into a dry flood plain.

21

'This is it, kids,' Gary informed them happily, pulling up outside the Inglewood's new home. It was there that they would be staying for the next few months. 'Just like in the photographs my boss showed me.'

Amanda's smile was as exaggerated as her husband's, and, like him, she was hoping it would be contagious. They were staring at Audrey, not at Billy, because she was the one who needed convincing. Her little brother didn't mind where he was, as long as he had comics to read and his bicycle to ride.

'It looks fabulous!' Audrey's eyes opened wide in sarcastic excitement, and she forced her mouth into a gaping smile.

For his part, Gary found the house very charming. A long verandah overlooked a parched lawn and wild flower shrubs. The hammock strung between two ghost gums was begging for him to crawl inside and stretch out after the longest road-trip he'd undertaken since university; Brisbane to nowhere in a day and a half.

'Billy, how about you put your comic book down for a minute?' Gary suggested. 'You want to check out the house, don't you?'

He tore his attention away from the radio-active tyrannosaurus skeleton's nocturnal museum rampage and, pushing himself up as high as he could, peered out the car window.

'Cool!'

They all got out and stretched their arms and legs.

'Where are the keys, Gary?'

'I knew I'd forgotten something.' He frowned.

'You did *not.*'

'Dad?' Audrey's voice sounded worried.

'Calm down, girls.' He laughed. 'The property belongs to a local who runs the corner shop. Did you happen to see the shop across from the post office, Mandy?'

'I did. How about I take Billy down there to get the keys and buy some lunch while you two start piling our cherished belongings on the verandah?'

'No problem. Tell him the key is for Gary...'

'Yeah, I know,' Amanda cut him off. 'Gary Inglewood, geologist with the CSIRO.'

He just smiled.

'Are you walking or riding, Billy?' his mum asked as she stuck his hat on his head.

His eyes narrowed and he stared at the big blue sky, as though he'd been requested to answer an existential conundrum. Amanda always said he must have inherited that from his father.

Gary opened the boot and removed Billy's little bike. He knew what his son's answer would be.

'I think I'll ride.'

By the time Amanda and Billy had returned to the house, Gary and Audrey had finished unpacking the car.

Audrey was swinging lazily in the hammock after having her dad evict a spider that had already claimed it as his squat. She'd wanted him to kill it, but Gary had explained that it had a role to play in the ecosystem and was particularly helpful in reducing the fly population.

'How was your first walk to the Isisford corner shop?' Gary asked as he swept dirt and leaves from the five steps that led up to the verandah.

'It was very quiet. Ken, the owner, is a friendly chap, and Billy met one of the local boys.'

'Is that right? Did he want to know where we were from, and what we were doing in town?'

'No,' Amanda frowned. 'In fact, he was a little strange. He asked Billy how old he was, and when he told him he was nearly six, the boy just smiled and walked away whistling.'

'Strange,' Gary agreed. 'I'm tired. I think I'll have a little nap.'

'That's a good idea. We could all do with some rest, couldn't we, Billy?'

He nodded.

The Inglewood's nap lasted until nightfall.

Three shadowy forms reached the porch of Isisford's tiny white church just as the clouds burst.

Stumpy Davidson looked up at the night sky, and a flash of lightning illuminated his weather-worn face.

Distant thunder echoed across the surrounding plains.

'The rains 'ave come back at last,' he muttered. His voice was troubled.

Isaac Krump shone the torch on the keyhole while his brother slid the key in.

'That's the way, Larry. Give 'im a good twist.'

The door clicked and swung open. The sound of the torrential downpour was even louder inside. Raindrops were pounding against the church's corrugated iron roof.

Larry felt around for a switch, flicked it, and the three men were temporarily blinded by the light.

'It doesn't seem that long ago we were preparing the last conversion.'

'Ten years already,' Stumpy mused. 'The older you get, the faster the bloody sand pours through the hourglass.'

'Ten years,' Isaac repeated. 'Not to the day, but to the very week all the same. The rains started a little earlier last time, didn't they?'

The others nodded as they began removing bibles from the pews.

'It sure is a blessing to have this new family in town. How long have they been here now?'

'About a month,' Isaac said.

'I haven't seen them at church,' Larry added, a hint of reproach in his voice.

'No. They're not god-fearing folk.' Stumpy was now packing the hymn books in a pile beside the door.

'So, they still don't know about the conversion?'

Stumpy shook his head.

'Who's going to tell them before the time comes?' Larry asked.

'That's none of our concern, Larry. Brother Jacob will take care of that,' Stumpy warned him.

'I know, but how can we be sure they'll do what's required of them? What if they refuse?'

The three men stopped working. Nobody spoke. Only the rain hammering down filled the silence.

'That hasn't happened for seventy years,' Stumpy reminded them solemnly. 'I can barely remember it, and I'm grateful for that. I was only a kid at the time. Dad was away at war against the Japs, like all the other men of fightin' age. He never come back, he didn't. He never seen what happened to Isisford. Even today, I dunno who was the lucky ones, them who come back or them who didn't.'

'The Inglewoods will do their bit for the community, one way or another.' Isaac pointed to the big wooden cross screwed to the wall at the far end of the church. 'Help me get that down, brother.'

The effect of the previous night's deluge was immediate. The Inglewood's desiccated lawn had thirstily soaked up the liquid godsend and was already turning green. It was a Saturday morning and Gary was sitting on the verandah, sipping a coffee and thinking about his research project. Billy was madly racing around the yard on his bike. He'd already come off once and cut his knee on a rusty nail that was sticking out of one of the house's stumps, but that hadn't deterred him.

'Good morning,' a voice called from the street. Gary saw a middle-aged couple standing at the wire gate. It seemed they had been waiting patiently for him to notice them, and now they were waiting to be invited in. They were different from the other townsfolk. Perhaps they were outsiders. In a town with just over two hundred residents, he thought he knew every face by now. This couple had more the appearance of university professors than country folk. They had an air of eccentricity about them. In fact, they looked like complete and utter nutcases.

The man wore a pith hat that overshadowed a skeletal face with sunken eyes. It was a face that looked more accustomed to dim monasteries than the vast and sun-drenched Queensland bush. A silk foulard was wrapped around his scrawny neck, and long beige socks and sandals covered his stickman legs. He looked like Nick Cave dressed up as Doctor Livingstone for some kind of freakish fancy dress party.

His wife wore a long exotic gown and was adorned with fantastic golden jewellery that swirled under her ears and slithered along what little bare skin could be seen at the base of her neck.

They both carried books and leaflets in their hands.

Gary suddenly realised they must be bible bashers, come to convert him from his Darwin-loving scientist ways.

'Mr Inglewood, I presume.' The man called out in a high-pitched, academic voice.

Doctor Livingstone, I presume. Gary thought, but did not venture the joke.

'Yes, that's right.'

'We were wondering if we could speak to you. My name is Professor Jacob Fisher. This is my wife, Professor Deirdre Fisher.'

'Nice to meet you,' Gary lied.

Deirdre looked down at the closed gate, then stared sternly at Gary. The message could not have been clearer.

'Sorry,' Gary said. 'Where are my manners? Please, come in before it starts raining again.'

'Thank you. The powers-that-be certainly did unleash a powerful downfall last night.'

Damn! Gary thought. *I left that door wide open for him. Strange that he said "powers-that-be" and not "the Good Lord" though.*

'Hello, young soldier,' Professor Jacob Fisher said as Billy came speeding around a corner. He came to a grinding halt at the visitor's sandalled feet.

'Hello. That's a nice hat.'

Gary felt like laughing, but held it in.

'Thank you, I bought it in Kenya. That's in Africa.'

'Cool!'

'Did you hurt your leg?'

'Yeah, I cut it on a nail. It didn't hurt though.'

'Poor little thing.' Deirdre, who gave the impression of being a rather strict woman despite her almost bohemian dress sense, smiled sympathetically at Billy.

'You are a brave young soldier, aren't you?' Jacob continued.

'Yes, sir.'

'That's good. You need to be brave living here in Isisford.'

'So, you are locals? I haven't seen you here before,' Gary asked.

They walked ceremoniously up to the verandah, and Gary signalled for them to take a seat.

'That is correct, Mr Inglewood. We've been researching overseas for some time, in the Middle East. We, like you, are scholars.'

'Biblical scholars, I take it?'

They looked at each other for a moment, as though in silent communication.

'We do dabble in biblical archaeology from time to time. However, our main field of interest is in far more ancient and, dare I say, powerful beliefs.'

Gary was taken aback. He hadn't been expecting this.

'The Mesopotamians?'

'Yes. They intrigue us above all. Theirs was a great civilisation, and their knowledge of the universe was profound.'

'You want to talk to me about the religious beliefs of the ancient world?'

Professor Jacob Fisher removed his pith hat and placed it on his lap.

'Yes, we do. Have you been to church recently, Mr Inglewood? Here in Isisford?'

'No, I haven't. I must admit I'm not a very good Christian. In fact, I'm not a Christian at all.'

'You believe only in that which can be measured and explained; in that which obeys the empirical laws of scientific knowledge.'

'That about sums it up.'

'That isn't a problem for the moment. We too seek to understand that which seems beyond comprehension, to clear a path through the fog that lies between our petty minds and the fabric that lines and defines our universe. Do not forget, Mr Inglewood, that men like Da Vinci and Newton didn't content themselves to allow previous laws to control their curiosity. Their great minds roamed free of such man-made bonds and shackles.'

Gary said nothing. They had his attention, and they knew it.

'We have much to tell you, and now is not the appropriate time. You should know, however, that the church has been temporarily converted.'

'The church has been converted? You've got to be pulling my leg?' Gary stood up and looked out to the street, trying to find the hidden cameras. 'How can you convert a church? You can't just change from worshipping one God to another according to your mood.'

The professors smiled condescendingly, and then they said simultaneously, 'You are more Christian than you think, Mr Inglewood.'

'Tell me,' he continued. 'Why do the locals want to convert the church?'

'We convinced them to do so. Their faith in the existence of a monotheistic and jealous God wasn't as unshakeable as they pretended.'

Deirdre leaned forward and trapped Gary in her hypnotic gaze. She looked more like a gypsy fortune-teller than a university professor. 'One could even say, Mr Inglewood, that the locals are more open-minded than you, changing their opinions as new evidence emerges.'

'So, you convinced the town to temporarily change from one set of beliefs to another by presenting them with some kind of irrefutable proof?'

'Precisely,' Jacob answered. It was as simple as that.

Gary's lips parted again as more questions formed in his mind. *How did you do that? Why is the conversion only temporary? Above all, what is this other god like and how is he worshipped?*

'As I said, Mr Inglewood, this is not the appropriate time. We have

28

much to do. We'll be in touch we you.'

Without further ado, the professors took their leave.

Gary's first impression of his visitors had been that they were nutcases. The resulting conversion should have confirmed this. But as they closed the wire gate and walked away, like friends who had just dropped by to chat about the weather, he found himself wondering whether maybe, just maybe, there'd been some sense in what they had told him.

Amanda and the children ate their dinner uninterestedly while Gary recounted the morning's events. Amanda just shook her head and rolled her eyes.

'Mum. Mum.'

'Daddy's talking, Billy.'

'Can I leave the table?'

'Yes, honey.'

She turned her attention to Audrey, reading her daughter's thoughts.

'You're not hungry?'

'No, not really.'

Ever since their arrival, Gary had been trying to get his daughter to make an effort to fit in and feel comfortable in Isisford. With the latest turn of events, he knew any further attempts would be futile.

'Sweetie.' She hated being called that, she was nearly twelve years old, but old habits die hard. 'Have you heard any talk at school, or at the pool, or anywhere, about the conversion of the church?'

She shook her head.

'No strange talk at all?'

She gave him a nasty look.

'Dad, there's *only* strange talk here. But luckily for me, nobody has mentioned the church, or conversions, or crazy cults in my presence.'

The iron roof began to sing as rain fell heavily.

'It's raining again,' Gary mused.

'The rain. That's what everybody keeps going on about,' Audrey added.

'Well, that's normal talk, isn't it?' Amanda said.

'I suppose, but a lot of them have been saying that it will stop in a few days. On Friday afternoon, I heard one of the fathers telling his son that the rain was a lot heavier than it had been ten years ago and that once it stopped there would be a massive plague.'

'What sort of plague?'

'I have no idea. Like I said, there's only strange talk around here.'

Gary bit his lower lip, then just shook his head, as though chasing a preposterous thought away.

'It sounds strange to us, but the locals know this land and understand how weather extremities can impact upon it.'

Overhead, the rain intensified.

Gary grabbed a Snickers bar and put it on the counter next to the newspaper, milk, Weetbix, and loaf of wholegrain bread. It was his reward for doing the pre-breakfast grocery run.

Ken looked at his customer's purchases intensely, as though preparing himself for a memory test, then adjusted his glasses and tapped away at his old cash register.

'Fourteen dollars, please.'

Gary handed him the money.

'Perfect. So, what do you have planned for today?'

'Oh, nothing special. Maybe we'll go for a drive later on and have a picnic near the river. We often do that on Sundays.'

'That sounds nice, doesn't it?' He put the shopping into a bag for him, smiling sympathetically. 'You need to enjoy these family moments together while you can.'

Gary nodded politely.

'I think it's very admirable...'

'Ken!' It was his wife, listening in on their conversation from the backroom.

He turned around, startled, almost dropping the loaf of wholegrain, and she mouthed a warning.

Gary couldn't hear the words, but he heard the air escape from between the woman's panicked lips.

Ken handed him the bag and smiled, lips firmly closed.

'Are you going to church this morning?' Gary asked innocently.

He shook his head. It seemed he was refusing to speak. He reached down and took another Snickers from the chocolates shelf in front of the counter.

'No church this morning,' he explained simply. 'Here, give this one to Billy.'

'Thanks. That's very kind of you.'

'Not at all, neighbour.'

The riverside picnic ended up being called off. Although it looked as though the rain had stopped for the day, the ground was still soaking wet from the downpour. Gary was also worried the river might burst its banks all of a sudden. The water was flowing fast as it was, and the flood plain at the end of their street had changed from a dry expanse of dormant grass stems to a muddy lake.

They had lunch on the verandah instead, listening to the only radio station that could be picked up in the area.

Gary lit the gas barbecue and oiled the grill as Slim Dusty sang *Under the Spell of Highway One*, accompanied by an orchestra of static.

'Daddy.' Audrey used her little girl voice, the one she knew would touch a soft spot in his heart.

'Yes, sweetheart.'

'We need to talk.'

Gary had heard that one from his wife a few times, but it was the first time his little angel had used it on him.

'Let me guess. You want to leave Isisford?'

She nodded. 'Is it possible?'

Gary sighed as he opened a packet of lamb and rosemary sausages.

'I have to stay here for a while. I have to finish my work. Can't you hold on just a little longer, sweetie? I promise I'll never ask you to leave the city again if you can just be brave and hold on a little longer.'

'Promise?'

'I promise.' He looked her in the eyes and put his hand over his heart, leaving a greasy palm print on his white T-shirt.

'Audrey,' her mother called to her. 'Come and help me cut some pineapple. Busy hands calm a worried mind.'

'That was one of granny's sayings, mum. You stole it.'

'Yes, I did. Now it's one of mine, and some day, it will be one of yours too.'

'Hello, Mr Inglewood.'

It was Professor Fisher, alone this time.

Gary looked at his wife and she nodded in recognition. There was no need to introduce the unwelcome visitor. Amanda could tell the stranger fit the description her husband had given her the night before. He was a freakish skinny man wearing a pith hat and knee-high socks.

'I have no intention of disturbing your lunch,' he informed the Inglewoods, as though reading their minds. 'I would just like to have a quick word with you, Mr Inglewood.'

Gary put his tongs down and went to the front gate. He exchanged a few words with the professor and they bid each other farewell. The visitor left as discreetly as he'd appeared.

As much as he disliked it, Gary took time off from his research on Monday morning and walked over to the Isisford church for the first time.

He quickly realised that he wasn't alone. Many of the town's inhabitants were heading towards the small wooden building. Its white painted walls and porch shone bright like a beacon on that sunny morning. Gary noticed there was no white cross standing above the porch, and supposed it had been removed for the conversion, if indeed there had ever been one at all.

Once he'd arrived at the entrance to Isisford's holy sanctuary, he heard a humming sound coming from within. At first, he wondered if the small church housed an enormous beehive, but as he drew closer, the humming became clearer. It became human voices.

The church was crowded, almost to capacity. The entire adult population must have been there. They wore glorious scarlet robes that hung down to their feet. There were two hundred or so pious worshippers, but whom exactly did they worship?

'Mr Inglewood!' Professor Fisher clasped his hands over those of the newcomer. His robe was the most splendid of them all, adorned with golden trimmings, and a brooch in the shape of an insect of some kind. Gary noticed he'd forgotten his pith hat.

'We're glad that you've come.' He looked around at the congregation, making it clear that he was speaking on behalf of all, and indeed all other mouths had ceased to speak. Their undivided attention was focused on Gary and the professor.

'Do you see the splendour of our church, of *your* church, Mr Inglewood?'

He looked around. It was undeniably splendid. Strangely beautiful tapestries adorned the walls, and golden ornaments hung from the ceiling.

It was also unsettling. Gary had never been a religious man. His atheist father had sent him to the Double Helix young scientists' club instead of Sunday school. For him, religion and science were incompatible. Obviously, Professor Fisher was not of the same opinion. However, even for an atheist like Gary, the shock of seeing the changes to the church made him feel uneasy. It seemed so profoundly blasphemous.

Where the cross should have been, behind the pulpit, an enormous idol hung from the wall. The son of man had been replaced with a hideous creature whose fangs, leathery wings, and claws contrasted disturbingly with Christ's lovingly sorrowful countenance.

'It looks like a demon!' Gary had meant it as a thought, but the silence around him and the bemused look on Professor Fisher's face confirmed his fear that he'd spoken aloud.

'I suppose you're right, Mr Inglewood. This is the Church of Asag, and he was indeed considered by the ancient Mesopotamians to be a ferocious demon, a terrible monster made of rock and magic.'

'What does the pastor think about this?'

'There is no pastor in Inglewood. There hasn't been one in a very long time. I carry out the religious services with the help of the congregation. Our church is one that shuns hierarchy.'

Yet despite his words, Gary was sure the professor pulled just about all of the strings in town.

'We convert the church to a house of worship honouring Asag every ten years, as the rainy season hits Isisford.'

Every ten years.

'Is Asag a god of plagues?'

The congregation murmured and Professor Fisher smiled, surprised and pleased by Gary's intuition.

'How do you know of Asag?'

He decided not to mention Audrey.

'I heard some talk of a plague every ten years.'

Professor Fisher lost his smile and scanned the crowd, seeking those who had spoken carelessly.

'These plagues are devastating, Mr Inglewood. You've seen how the land has changed over these past weeks. Land that was once dry and dead is now green and flourishing. It seems wonderful, but the wonder will be fleeting. Do you know what will come very shortly?'

'Locusts?' Gary guessed casually, shrugging his shoulders.

The crowd shuddered.

'Yes, Mr Inglewood, a terrible plague of locusts. Hell on Earth!'

Gary couldn't understand why the thought of a locust plague caused such dread. Then again, he knew little of such phenomena.

'We've avoided these plagues for many years, Mr Inglewood. You may find it difficult to believe, but the worship of Asag at this time, every ten years, protects us.'

'How do you worship him?'

The congregation was silent, and Gary could feel a heavy tension filling the church.

Professor Fisher told Gary about the ceremony, explaining what would take place, step by step, and he told him that it would need to be performed very soon. He solemnly informed Gary of his family's great responsibility.

'I understand. If this is what is required, it will be done. Asag will be honoured. I shall return home to my family and bring them back here immediately.'

The congregation bowed their heads as Gary strode respectfully from the Church of Asag.

'Gary, what are you doing?'

'You can ask questions later. Just get the car packed as quickly as possible!'

Billy came in from the yard, wondering what all the fuss was about.

'Get all your toys, honey,' Amanda told him, trying to sound calm.

'Are we going home?'

'Yes. Now get your toys quickly!'

'What about Audrey?'

'We'll get her from school before we leave.'

'Why are we leaving?'

Amanda looked at her husband, who was stuffing clothes into his suitcase. She'd never seen him rattled like this before. All of sudden, the foundations of her rational world began to shake.

'Daddy will explain everything later.'

'Billy!' Gary's voice thundered, as he tried to zip his bulging suitcase. 'Just – get – your – toys!'

Amanda turned on her husband angrily, about to spit out a volley of insults and complaints, letting him know he didn't have to yell at his son like that because he was already scared stiff. So was she, for that matter. But Gary looked at her, and she read his face. He was telling her she needed to trust him, and that if she did exactly what he told her to, everything would work out in the end.

She hurried to the wardrobe and pulled all of her clothes out, forcing her shaking hands to work as quickly as they could.

Billy dragged an armful of toys and comics onto the verandah.

'Billy, get off the verandah! Come inside!'

Amanda came rushing out of the bedroom with as much as she could carry.

'Gary, relax a little. It can't be that bad.'

'It bloody well can!'

He saw the fear in her eyes.

'Sorry.' He tried to calm himself down. 'Believe me, Mandy. It's bad. Just shove your stuff into the car.'

Billy started to cry.

'Be brave, Billy. Have you got all your toys?'

'Yes.'

Gary hauled his suitcase outside but ran into his wife as she rushed up onto the verandah.

'Gary,' she whispered. 'What happened at the church?'

He looked over her shoulder and saw why she'd been trying to get inside so urgently. The inhabitants of Isisford were swarming along the street. Professor Fisher piloted the stream of robed fanatics.

'Gary, you're planning on leaving are you?' The professor called out.

He opened the garden gate and approached the house. The others stayed outside, surrounding the station wagon, the Inglewood family's only means of salvation.

Gary slammed the front door closed, but he knew it was nothing more than a futile symbol of resistance.

Professor Fisher's voice sounded distant, even though he was already on the verandah. 'You lied to us, Mr Inglewood. You pretended to understand, but I could sense you were just trying to buy time. Worst of all, you have insulted Asag's holy name!'

'Go away, Fisher.'

'The youngest must be sacrificed, Mr Inglewood.'

Amanda shuddered. 'Did he say *sacrificed*?'

Gary nodded. 'Sacrificed to Asag.'

'Sacrificed – to – Asag,' she repeated, and would have laughed if

36

she hadn't known they were deadly serious. 'What has that got to do with us?'

'Everything!' Gary informed her. 'Billy is the youngest person in town.'

Billy was standing behind his parents, crying with confusion more than fear.

'We have to call the police!'

Gary shook his head. 'They won't have far to come, they're probably outside right now, blue uniforms replaced with long scarlet robes.'

'Open the door, Mr Inglewood. Ken doesn't want us to damage the house any more than necessary.'

'Leave us alone!' Amanda screamed as her maternal instinct kicked in.

'Be reasonable, Amanda,' Professor Fisher said soothingly. The sound of her name sent a shiver up her spine. 'We have Audrey, of course.'

'Don't you dare!' Gary was about two seconds away from opening the door, but his wife stilled his hand. Her fury hadn't yet smothered her reason.

'We have to get Audrey!'

'I know, but just slow down a little. If we go out there, it will all be over. We can't save Audrey if we get ourselves captured. It's not Audrey they want, it's B...' She stopped short. Billy was listening. 'We have the upper hand.'

Gary nodded and drew in a deep breath, trying to control his rage. His wife was right, despite her fear and anger, she'd managed to keep a relatively cool head.

'You're right, honey. But we can't stay in here for ever.'

A window shattered and shards sprayed into the house.

Billy's sobbing gave way to shrieks of pure terror.

There was no more time for contemplation. The townsfolk were about to storm the house.

Gary ran into the kitchen and grabbed a handful of carving knives. He'd never killed before, and was unsure he'd be capable of doing so now.

Scarlet robes pressed against the jagged opening that had been a window moments earlier.

'Don't be selfish!' they were saying. 'Think about what's best for the community!'

Gary slashed out, a knife in each hand, but the townsfolk jumped back just in time.

'You're just making it harder for yourself, Gary. Asag's demands must be obeyed. Who are you to refuse him?' Professor Fisher's voice came from somewhere on the verandah.

The figures closed in on the window once more. Familiar faces that had once been friendly were now frozen with determination. They were not hostile, not even nervous; they were simply the faces of men and women concentrated on doing their duty. It was terrifying.

Gary's knives slashed out again and the assailants stepped back, their frozen faces melting for a brief moment in time. Then they hesitated, preparing themselves for another attempt at getting through the window.

The blast of a shotgun rang out.

There was no telling where it had been aimed.

'Who did that?' Professor Fisher shouted angrily. 'Put that away, fool! The boy must be sacrificed to Asag. He's useless if you kill him first!'

Amanda put her trembling lips to her husband's ear as he considered stabbing at the maniacs who were coming towards the window again.

'Maybe we can sneak out the back,' she whispered.

The idea was so ridiculously simple.

'It might just work,' Gary admitted.

What they would do next was another matter. They would have to find Audrey without being caught by the brainwashed townsfolk. It was worth a try.

'We'll have to move quickly. Ready?'

Amanda nodded.

Gary picked Billy up, being careful not to cut him with the knives, and they made a run for the back door. Amanda swung it open with the prodigious strength a mother is capable of mustering when her little one is under threat.

Bright sunlight blinded them, and, for a dreadful moment, Gary and Amanda expected to feel desperate hands grasping at their hysterical son. Gary was ready to slash at them with his knives. These people with whom he'd been speaking on civil terms, from whom he'd bought groceries and petrol, and, worst of all, with whom he'd shared a beer, and now he was prepared to cut them up, one by one.

Their eyes soon adjusted to the light, but instead of finding a mob of fanatics blocking their path, they found the mortified face of one little girl.

'Audrey! How did...? Never mind. We have to go.' Gary's head turned from side to side like that of a hare spooked by a hungry fox. Within seconds, a flood of religious nuts would be swamping them from both sides of the house.

'Dad, they've gone.'

'What do you mean?'

'It's all over. They've all left. They let me go and ran away.'

'I don't understand.'

'Neither do I. They've just gone.'

Gary listened. He could no longer hear Professor Fisher's crazed voice, or the sound of breaking glass, or footsteps on the verandah. There was only silence, except for a distant humming.

Then he noticed something else, but couldn't quite put his finger on it.

'The light,' Amanda said. 'The sun has disappeared!'

The humming was growing louder.

Then the horrible noise was all around them.

Gary dropped his knives and passed Billy to Amanda, almost dropping him too. He fumbled in his pockets, but his hands were too shaky.

Audrey screamed. Her shrill voice was almost as loud as the

ominous humming, which was increasing in intensity with every passing second. It was Asag humming, Gary imagined. The ancient demon was deafening them with his sadistic tune.

The darkness kept growing.

Gary managed to pull his car keys out, and they jangled silently.

'Get in the car now!'

They ran around to the street, to where, just moments before, the townsfolk had been gathered, preparing to force their way into the house and seize the innocent child whose blood was to be shed for the greater good.

As the Inglewoods got into the car and slammed the doors, the dark cloud hit.

A hailstorm of locusts pounded the car. They slid down the windscreen and windows, scratching hopelessly at the smooth glass.

Audrey started to cry and checked nervously that all the windows were properly closed. Billy, on the other hand, had calmed down and was watching the onslaught with amazed amusement.

'Can you drive through this, honey?' Amanda asked.

Gary turned the key in the ignition and pumped the accelerator. He was shocked by what had happened, and a nagging question began to taunt his scientific mind. *Is this Asag?* He flicked the windscreen wipers on and sent a squadron of locusts catapulting off the car.

The scene that lay before the Inglewoods was appalling. Audrey's sobbing grew louder as she caught sight of the street swarming with insects. The inhabitants of Isisford had vanished, giving way to the seething mass.

Gary smiled uneasily as he put some music on. He wanted to drown out the nauseating sound he knew would be caused by rubber crushing thousands of exoskeletons.

The car lurched forwards, its windscreen wipers slashing like sabres. A trail of mangled insect shell and slime followed the Inglewoods as they left the town to its fate.

'Sit back and enjoy the ride, folks. Nothing, not even Asag, is going to stop us from getting back to Brisbane.'

OLD MABEL'S STRAY CAT

It was a cool night in late February. After a summer of violent thunderstorms and suffocating humidity, Mabel Atkinson was finally able to enjoy the comfort of milder weather. She went to bed early, just after nine o'clock, as was her custom, and read a short story from a collection by Ruth Rendell. As soon as she'd finished it, she placed the book on her bedside table and switched the lamp off. Then she curled herself up under the patchwork quilt that her sister had made for her the previous autumn. Thinking about the story she'd just read, she soon fell asleep.

Outside, all was quiet. The widow's neighbours knew she went to bed at a more than reasonable hour and showed their consideration by restricting any noisy activities or loud conversation. 'Don't make too much noise, Old Mabel is probably asleep already,' they would say.

It must have been around midnight that Old Mabel woke up. She often emerged from her slumber during the night due to the fact that she settled in so early. She would read a few more pages of her book or just sip some water while she admired the paintings of gnarled ghost gums and murky billabongs that adorned her living room walls. Back before Miss Pippins had lost her ninth life in a gruesome incident with the next-door neighbour's car, Old Mabel used to take advantage of her nocturnal awakening to check on her feline companion. Nowadays, she only had herself to look after.

But on that particular night, she had a creeping sort of feeling that something had roused her from her sleep. With the change in weather, she couldn't brush the cause off as being the humidity or the rumbling of distant thunder. She turned her bedside lamp on and considered reading another short story, but, before she could make a decision, she heard a sound coming from her front door.

Something – or somebody – seemed to be scratching at it.

She turned the lamp off again and crawled out of bed, then moved slowly towards the window so she could look out onto the doorstep. She pulled the curtains ever so slightly apart and peered outside, only to find there was nothing anywhere near the door. For a moment, she wondered whether it could have been a branch rubbing against the walls of her house, but she'd never noticed any before, and, at any rate, she didn't think the branches of the few trees in her front garden could have grown so rapidly as to suddenly touch her house.

Just as Old Mabel was about to let the curtain fall closed, she noticed a subtle movement near her letterbox. Something small and shadowy shifted. There was no doubt about it. It was the stealthy form of a cat.

'You poor little thing,' she whispered. 'You're all alone out there. You just want some shelter and a little company, don't you? Or perhaps some milk?'

The black silhouette of the cat's tail swished from side to side as though in response to Old Mabel's kind-hearted words, even though the creature couldn't possibly have heard her.

Old Mabel went to her kitchen and took a carton of milk from the refrigerator. There wasn't much left, but she figured she had just enough to give some to the cat without forsaking her Earl Grey in the morning. She poured some into a saucer and, just to show the stray cat she really was a generous soul, also removed some left-over tuna from the top shelf of the refrigerator.

'There you go. That should help your plight a little.'

She took the supper out to the front doorstep and placed it to one side. There was no longer any sign of the cat, but she knew what they were like, always wandering back and forth. It would find her gift.

Proud of her good deed, Old Mabel closed the door and went back to bed.

She went outside first thing in the morning and took a deep breath of fresh air. Looking down, she smiled broadly. The saucers were empty. They had been licked clean with the strokes of a precise and appreciative tongue, not a drop of milk or a morsel of tuna had been neglected.

Later that day, when she went to the shops with Lisa Stadley from next door, her younger neighbour didn't fail to notice that Mabel had put an unusually large quantity of two aliments in her trolley.

'Why so much milk and tuna, Mrs Atkinson? If you need some help with your groceries, don't hesitate to ask. I know it isn't easy living on the pension. My parents have to watch their budget carefully.'

'Goodness,' Old Mabel laughed. 'That's not it at all, dear. It's just that a little puss visited last night. I put some milk and tuna out for it, and it was all gone this morning. I feel sorry for the poor thing.'

Lisa shook her head approvingly. 'You are a sweetie, Mrs Atkinson. Don't tell Peter about your little friend though. You know how he dislikes cats.'

Old Mabel knew all too well. She sometimes wondered whether the Miss Pippins incident had really been an accident. Lisa probably didn't know about that though. Old Mabel hadn't had the heart to tell her about what had happened, and she doubted Peter had told his wife about it either.

'I'm too old to care about what people think, dear, but I won't mention the matter if you'd rather Peter didn't know. I don't want to upset him.'

'It will be our little secret then!' Lisa chirped.

Old Mabel put a finger to her lips, and the two women giggled like girls.

All the following week, she put a dish of milk and a dish of tuna out for the stray cat. On Wednesday night, she woke up and thought she could hear the little feline's tongue lapping. She got out of bed and opened the door, hoping to usher her unofficial pet inside, but by the time she got there, she found nothing except for two immaculately empty dishes.

'You are a timid one, aren't you? Just don't let that Peter Stadley catch you, whatever you do!'

She glanced towards the house next door. Lisa was a darling and the children weren't too bad as far as could be expected for their spoilt generation, but Peter Stadley didn't deserve them. He reminded her of her late husband, for all the wrong reasons and none of the right ones.

'Stay away from him, little kitty!' she whispered into the cool night air. She thought she heard a meow in reply but couldn't see where the cat was. All the same, it reassured her that her message had got through.

Old Mabel continued putting milk and tuna out for the stray, and every morning, without fail, she was pleased to find that her offering had been gratefully accepted. Whenever she woke up during the night, she crept over to the door and opened it as discreetly as possible, hoping to catch the cat unawares and coax it inside for a hug and a warm place to sleep. But she never succeeded. The animal must have been both very astute and terribly shy. Once, after opening the door, she saw that there was some milk left in the dish, but it was all gone when she checked the next morning. After that, she gave up on trying to surprise the cat in the middle of the night. All the same, she decided it needed a name, and one in particular sprang to mind. Phantom.

One Friday morning, when Old Mabel opened the door, she didn't smile. Instead, she let out a terrible wail that would have put a banshee to shame. Lying in her front garden with a portable cage in his lifeless right hand was Peter Stadley. The cage had obviously been intended for Old Mabel's stray cat, but the nasty man had been beaten at his game. His face was pale and grotesque, and wide gashes made his cheeks look like bloody gills. His throat had been ripped open and blood covered the path leading from the garden gate to the doorstep. It looked as though he'd been attacked by a tiger.

Old Mabel glanced at the two saucers. They were empty, as usual. She fainted.

Old Mabel woke up in bed. For a moment, she thought she'd slept in and that the sight of Peter lying dead in her front garden with a cat trap in hand had been nothing more than a vivid nightmare. But the presence of three people in her bedroom informed her that the macabre discovery of that morning had been all too real. A uniformed officer, a detective, and a stunned spectre that vaguely resembled Lisa Stadley were all at the foot of her bed.

'I'm so sorry, Lisa,' Old Mabel said timidly, her voice drenched with sadness. 'I had no idea that Phantom was capable of such mischief. I can hardly believe it!'

Lisa didn't move. She didn't even look up. She just continued staring at her feet.

'Phantom?' the detective asked, so intrigued by Old Mabel's apology that he neglected to introduce himself and his sergeant.

'Yes, my stray cat.'

The detective shot his sergeant a look that was as good as saying, 'She's obviously completely batty.'

'Mrs Atkinson, I can assure you that Mr Stadley was not murdered by a stray cat. I suspect a human being is behind this heinous crime.'

'But what about the cage?'

'He may very well have come onto your property in search of a stray cat with the intention of taking it away, perhaps to the RSPCA.

That amounts to trespass, since he obviously didn't have your permission. But that's beside the point now, isn't it? Regardless, he certainly wasn't killed by a cat.'

The detective paused for a moment, and it was as though a dark veil had fallen across his face. Old Mabel knew he was thinking about the savage gashes that deformed Peter's face and throat. He was telling himself the old woman could almost be forgiven for thinking that a feline was responsible for the brutal killing.

'You really think so? Oh, I do hope you're right.'

'Can you think of anybody, any human, who might have wished him harm?'

'I don't think so. He wasn't the most pleasant fellow, but I don't think he had any enemies.' She glanced at Lisa, regretting her blunt words, but found her staring at the floor, a million miles away.

Silence fell like an executioner's axe as the detective pondered the situation. Then the sergeant, who'd been keeping quiet but analysing the facts of the case, whispered something in his superior's ear.

'You think there could be a connection?'

The sergeant nodded confidently.

'Very well. That's not a bad idea. If you're willing, and Mrs Atkinson agrees to it, then I think I can get that approved.'

'What idea?' Old Mabel asked.

The detective explained the plan to her.

Old Mabel woke up in the middle of the night to a frightful racket. The sergeant, who had been sleeping in the guest's room, was now in the front garden and yelling at somebody.

'What's happening?'

'Stay in bed, Mrs Atkinson!'

But she didn't obey. Instead, she stumbled out to the front door.

He was wearing his pyjamas and had his Taser drawn and aimed at the ground, near where Peter's corpse had been.

'Don't shoot Phantom. It's not his fault. He was just protecting himself from that cat hater!'

'I told you to stay inside! There's a dangerous criminal out here!'

A manlike voice meowed in protest. Old Mabel was sure she recognised it.

'You are not a cat! Put your hands on your head and don't move!'

Old Mabel followed the sergeant outside. She wanted to prevent him from hurting Phantom. As she stepped out, she noticed the two perfectly empty dishes at her feet.

The sergeant pulled a pair of clawed gloves off the filthy long-haired man kneeling on her garden path.

Old Mabel didn't understand what was happening. She flicked the switch that turned the outside light on so she could observe the creature more easily. A pair of green, feline eyes gleamed back at her. She knew what contact lenses were, but it didn't occur to her that this man was wearing any. The eyes were not angry or afraid, but quite simply confused, and, she couldn't help but think, they contained a hint of thankfulness as well.

'Stop breathing on me with your disgusting milk and tuna breath!' the sergeant snapped as he pulled the vagabond to his feet. He radioed for a patrol car to come and get them.

Old Mabel had never been so bewildered in all her life. She hadn't been feeding a stray cat after all, although the man seemed so much like one.

'Who is that strange man?'

'He's your stray cat, Mrs Atkinson. I had a feeling this nutcase was behind it all. I've heard reports about a man who believes he's a cat prowling through the city and getting up to all kinds of antics. It wasn't until I came here yesterday that I realised he presented a danger to anyone but himself.'

The man meowed sadly.

'What are you going to charge him with, Sergeant?'

It was the policeman's turn to feel bewildered. 'Well, with murder, of course. He must have caught your neighbour walking onto your property with a cat trap for your so-called stray and attacked him. Poor Mr Stadley must have had one hell of a fright when he discovered he would need a much bigger cage than the one he'd brought.'

Old Mabel looked at the travesty of a human being. As terrifying as the maniac was with his gleaming eyes and feline behaviour, she couldn't help shake off the notion that he was still her poor little Phantom.

'Don't arrest it, Sergeant. Peter was trespassing. This stray was just enjoying the humble treats I'd left for it. It was just obeying its instincts by defending itself. Please, let it go!'

A patrol car arrived at the kerb outside Old Mabel's house, its blue and red lights flashing but its siren off.

'Mrs Atkinson, I'll send our police counsellor around to have a chat with you at her earliest convenience.'

The sergeant shepherded the detainee into the police car, then took his place beside his colleague. From the back seat, a loud melancholic meow reached Old Mabel's ears.

VERONICA'S DOGS

'You have often asked me about cases of species dysphoria, Charles.'

Charles Radic closed his copy of the Australian Journal of Psychology and dropped it onto his desk. He'd been under the tutelage of Professor Broughton for nearly five years and knew when the University of Queensland's most highly regarded expert on psychosis was about to say something memorable.

'If I tell you a secret, will you promise to keep your lips sealed?'

Radic grinned. His tutor had a taste for the dramatic. 'Of course.'

Professor Broughton took a bottle of Lagavulin from the small cabinet beside his desk and poured two glasses.

'Last year, after several complaints from residents living near Bowman Park in Bardon, police arrested a man. He'd been acting strangely and sleeping in the rushes along the banks of Ithaca Creek. More bizarrely still, he'd been coming into the yards of homeowners who had dogs and eating from their bowls. One resident even caught him marking his territory.'

'You can't be serious?' Radic asked, the repugnant thought causing his brow to crease and his nose to flare up.

'But I am.'

'What became of him?'

'The authorities reacted intelligently for a change and a media circus was avoided. The man was given expert attention. I can vouch for that.'

Radic clasped his hands together in front of his mouth, the tips of his index fingers touching his nose. This was bound to be the most intriguing tale Professor Broughton had ever shared with him, and that was saying a lot.

'It would be an exaggeration to claim that this chap is now of sound mind, or that he ever was or will be. But he has certainly returned to the human race, for whatever that's worth.'

'What a strange case!'

'It is indeed, and you don't know the half of it yet,' the professor continued as he took a few sheets of paper from the bottom drawer of his desk. 'Would you allow me to read his account of the incident that led to the onset of dysphoria?'

'I'm all ears,' Radic answered.

'These are the patient's words. He's very articulate and his honesty is admirable. This account will prove to be an invaluable aid in comprehending the mind of a dysphoric individual. I have, of course, changed his name to protect his identity, and in order to avoid placing your good self in a compromising position. For his part, he refused to reveal the identity of the woman involved, despite the insistence of his therapists. Arguably, she's in even greater need of attention than he is.'

'Understood,' Radic said, although his choice of word was clearly inappropriate given the context.

With that, Professor Broughton began.

This is my account of the events leading to my psychotic episode. I've changed the names of the people involved and refuse to reveal their identities even to you, my therapist. After all, you're the one who has made me realise that nobody else is responsible for what happened to me. I should also point out that the wording of the exchanges reported in this account is not exact, but I've done my best to present the details of my experience as accurately as possible.

I first saw the woman I will call Veronica at a café in Bardon one Saturday morning after cycling with my friend and neighbour, Anders. We'd stopped, as was our weekend ritual, for a flat white after a vigorous ride. I'd never been to that particular café before, but I was to make the mistake of returning there on innumerable occasions over the following months.

While Anders was ordering our coffees at the counter, I noticed a dignified woman in an immaculate white and violet tracksuit sitting at a table by the door. What struck me about her at first wasn't her beauty, or the way her dark shoulder-length hair looked as though it had just been coiffed when it was obvious she'd been jogging, but the fact that her dog, a handsome and proud boxer, was sitting opposite her as though they were engaged in conversation.

My reaction was immediate and intense, one that I suppose romantics would have classified as love at first sight. But I'm no romantic, and I now know that this feeling was far more complicated and inexplicable than any classical *coup de foudre*. As it happened, her appearance and the fact that she was treating her pet like a person greatly aggravated me. Although I'm no stranger to middle-class snobbery myself, it was her air of pretentiousness that annoyed me so much about this woman. Every perfectly placed hair and every drop of perspiration that she dabbed from her forehead with a violet handkerchief screamed arrogance and vanity. Then, before my very eyes, she poured two glasses of water and placed one in front of her canine companion.

It was ridiculous and incongruous. I found myself both despising and desiring this strange woman, and I have to admit, if I'm to be completely honest with you, that I had an overriding urge to give her a good spanking right there in the café.

Little did I know at that confounding moment that another surprise was in store. On his way back from the counter, Anders stopped at her table and spoke to her. He patted the dog's head, and I noticed her grimace, momentarily creasing her regal brow. Then he pointed at me, and I felt my whole body tighten as she stared straight into my eyes. I felt exposed.

A second later, she turned back to Anders and flashed him a fake smile.

It wasn't until my friend was sitting opposite me that I managed to tear my gaze away from the woman.

'Who's that?' I asked him as flatly as I could.

He told me her name and informed me that he'd invited her over for a drink that very evening. Anders' circle of friends was as wide as the Nullarbor Plain, and it was unusual that I failed to make a new acquaintance whenever I attended one of his parties. Still a bachelor in my mid-thirties, Anders and his fiancée were accustomed to my need to flirt with any single woman amongst their friends, and I had, on several occasions, gone home with fellow partygoers.

'I can see she has caught your attention,' my friend whispered.

'Is it that obvious?'

Anders gave me a hard cold stare and then glanced quickly at Veronica.

'I regret inviting her now. I should have known better. She's an interesting girl and can be a lot of fun in small doses, but you don't want to get too close.'

'You know I like them quirky,' I reminded him.

'Listen, just trust me on this. I'm warning you,' he continued. 'Stay away from this one, mate. She's messed up. She's the kind of girl you can have a laugh with over a drink, but nothing more.'

It was clear by his stern tone and stony expression that his words were to be taken seriously. But it was too late. I was infatuated.

For the first time since we'd become friends, which was close to six years, I was angry at Anders. I was aware of how ludicrous it was, but his words had deeply offended me, as though he'd spoken about a woman I'd known intimately for years. I've never been married, and expect I never will be fit to take on such a commitment, but I imagined a husband would react the same way to criticism aimed at his beloved wife.

I turned to look at Veronica and found her sipping at a cup of coffee and flicking through the morning newspaper. She stopped at one page and frowned. Then she spun the paper around and showed it to her dog, raising her razor-thin eyebrows, silently asking her pet for his opinion of the article. It was so deliciously ridiculous of her, and an uncontrollable urge came over me again.

Anders clicked his fingers at me, and my head snapped back toward him. He flinched, half expecting me to lash out at him. His eyes widened and he shook his head.

'Don't do this, mate. Get a grip,' he whispered desperately. 'You don't want to go there.'

I closed my eyes and nodded, but didn't mean it.

That night, at Anders' place, I wasn't myself. Or so he kept telling me. He told me to knock it off and have some fun, but I just kept asking him where Veronica was and by nine-thirty decided that my suspicions were true. Surely, he'd called her and retracted the invitation.

'Tell me the truth, mate,' I said once I'd drained yet another bottle of Byron Bay lager. 'You told her not to come, didn't you?'

'I did,' he admitted. 'Now, just forget about her. I wish I hadn't even spoken to her this morning. I should have known this would happen. You always do this.'

'What's that supposed to mean?' I hissed.

'You always go for the wrong types. That's what it means. You'll never have a serious relationship if you keep doing that.'

'Wrong type? Maybe I'm a wrong type too!'

'No, you're not. You're my mate, and you're a good bloke. I don't want to lose you.'

'So, that's how it is!' I practically yelled. 'I have to choose, do I?'

A dozen faces turned to see what all the commotion was about.

'You don't have to choose, mate. I just want you to make the right decision.'

'Don't worry, I will!'

But I didn't. I stormed out of the house and have barely spoken a word to Anders since that evening. I hope, one day, to make contact with him again. I know he wants to remain my friend and help me recover, but I'm so ashamed of myself.

After leaving the party, I walked from Anders' home in Ashgrove up to the hilltop suburb of Bardon. You've told me Anders tried to find me that night, knowing where I'd gone. He must have got behind the wheel despite being over the alcohol limit, but I didn't see his silver Land Rover. The poor fellow, I've put him through so much. I'll apologise to him one day, once I can bring myself to do it properly.

I crept into people's gardens and peered through lit windows. The suburb is a vast one, and the notion that I could be so lucky as to stumble upon Veronica simply by sneaking around like some kind of pervert was absolutely ridiculous. However, I was barely aware that I no longer belonged to the world of the sane. I reassured myself that anybody who felt love or lust for another was beyond sanity, and that I wasn't alone.

Needless to say, my foray was unsuccessful. I came close to being caught by one woman who heard her verandah floorboards creak as I approached a window. The front door lock turned before I had time to stumble down the steps that separated the verandah from the garden path, but I could just make out a man's voice telling her it was only possums and not to be so paranoid all the time. She must have accepted his advice, because the door remained closed.

In another yard, facing Ithaca Creek, I came close to being mauled by a German shepherd. I'd jumped a fence after noticing a woman who might have been Veronica washing dishes at a side window. The dog barked once and then came racing out of nowhere. It was almost on top of me before I'd even caught sight of it. I was terrified and thought my time had come. But for some reason — and looking back, this was the first sign of my dysphoria — when the animal growled at me, my instinct was to take a step toward it and growl right back at it. Indeed, I think I roared. The dog came to a halt within striking distance of my face, cocked its head in confusion, and then actually started backing away. I did the same, backing slowly away until I reached the front gate and could make a hasty departure.

My recollection of what happened then is unclear, but I must have decided to go home, because I woke up in bed the next morning. I was still fully dressed and my clothes were covered in leaves, prickles, and dirt. My legs ached terribly. My muscles were used to cycling long distances, but not to walking, crawling, and jumping.

I took a quick shower and decided to drive, not ride, to the café in

Bardon, hoping against all hope that Veronica would be there and that I would know what to say to her. But she wasn't, and after almost two hours and too many flat whites, I went home heartbroken.

I returned to the café on Monday morning, on the way to work, but Veronica wasn't there. I tried again on Tuesday morning, but the result was the same. I decided instead to cycle the streets of Bardon every evening that week, searching for a dark-haired princess with a boxer. I was pathetic, I was miserable, and I was unsuccessful.

Then, on Saturday morning, the first I hadn't spent with Anders in a long time, I rode to the café.

No sooner had I arrived at the door than I saw Veronica, dressed in a red tracksuit and gingerly dipping a jam drop into her mug of coffee. Her hair was perfect, shining in the warm morning sunlight that flooded through the doorway as though directing customers toward the counter. The boxer was sitting opposite, his posture as elegant as that of his owner, and he wore a studded collar that was the exact same shade of red as Veronica's tracksuit. It was all absurdly gorgeous.

I was simultaneously enthralled and aggravated by her all over again. I felt my knees buckle. She'd weakened them. She'd done what some of the toughest cycle paths in the state had been unable to do. I was like putty, but I didn't know whether she would want me in her hands.

She recognised me and twitched the corners of her lips. It wasn't exactly a smile, but it wasn't a frown either. The boxer looked at me too, with complete disinterest, the way he might watch a leaf fall from a tree.

I gathered up enough courage to speak to her. 'Hello,' I said. 'You didn't come to Anders' party last week.'

She seemed surprised. 'He told me there was a problem and he'd had to cancel it!'

'Oh, did he?' I said, shaking my head.

'What a dick!' she hissed, yet she managed to make those crude words sound quite classy.

'Can I buy you a coffee?'

'Thank you. That's very kind. But no,' she answered. 'I'm here with Bruce.'

She must have noticed my shock, because she practically scowled at me. What kind of excuse was that for not accepting an offer? And what kind of a name for a dog was Bruce? I wanted to slap her square across her pretty face. I wanted to chain bloody Bruce to an awning post outside the café and have my way with the princess right there in front of him. I wanted to teach her not to be so weird, and to teach her dog not to sit on chairs in cafés.

'Are you sure?' I asked, trying hard to remain civil.

'Yes, it was nice meeting you. You seem like a decent person, for a cyclist.'

Fuming, I turned around and left the café before I ended up doing something I would regret.

I rode around the block several times, and when I saw her leave, I followed her home.

You can't begin to imagine how relieved I was to see that she had Bruce on a lead, although the fact it was the exact same shade of red as his collar and her tracksuit made it look more like a fashion accessory than a means of control. Bruce walked by her side, not in front or behind, and didn't stop to sniff at the base of power poles or trees. He trotted along with the same air of calm self-satisfaction as his owner.

Veronica's posture was perfect. Her hair swung from side to side like a pendulum, and the tight mounds of her buttocks bobbed up and down hypnotically with every step she took. Her pace was so quick that I was able to follow quite comfortably on my bicycle without losing balance.

I won't give details of the location, but when she arrived at her house, I watched from behind a tree as she jogged up the front stairs and onto the verandah. She unleashed the dog and slipped her red trainers off before reaching into the pocket of her hoodie and removing the keys to the house. She unlocked three doors. The first was a wrought-iron grill, the second a security door with a fly screen, and the third a solid wooden door. She was obviously an anxious woman, locking three doors just to go for a jog and a coffee, and that provoked an even stronger desire in me to continue pursuing her. It wasn't the dog she needed to keep her safe and sound. It was me. She needed me to make sure she didn't fall victim to a rapist or a pervert.

I know what you're thinking, and you're quite right, of course. However, at that point in time, the irony of my situation was lost on me. I failed to realise that stalking a woman wasn't normal behaviour for a man who had always considered himself both law-abiding and of sound mind. Likewise, the cognitive dissonance — a term you have taught me — of fantasising about protecting a woman while feeling a barely controllable urge to take her by force failed to dawn on me until recent weeks.

Once Veronica and her dog had gone inside, I heard a low whimper and found myself looking behind me, half expecting to find a stray puppy. Of course, there was nothing and nobody. I was alone in the street.

My bladder was full, so I urinated against the tree, and then I got back on my bike and rode home.

My intention had been to resist the urge to go back to Veronica. But I couldn't. The thought of going to bed without catching another glimpse of her filled me with a kind of heavy emptiness.

As the sun sank behind Mount Coot-tha, I rode back to Bardon. It was already dark when I arrived in her street and hid my bike behind the tree I'd used as cover earlier that day. The air was cool and dark clouds threatened to empty their load on me, but I remained undeterred. I sniffed the air and was convinced I could smell her delicious perfume, the one she wore jogging for whatever reason. Of course, it must have been a figment of my increasingly incongruous imagination.

I was wearing my black cycling shorts and jersey so I wouldn't be easily spotted in the dark as I entered Veronica's garden and crept up to her house.

There was a light on around the back, but the house was up on stumps, and although there was a deck, there was no exterior staircase leading up to it.

I was going to have to climb.

After glancing up at the neighbour's house to make sure I wasn't being observed, I clambered up one of the steel posts that supported the deck and climbed over the railing. Making a quick escape wouldn't be easy, but I somehow hoped that if Veronica did catch me, she would be so kind as to invite me inside. A woman living by herself must get lonely sometimes and need a little company.

Stepping over to the window, being careful not to bump into the deck chair or empty washing basket and making sure I stayed out of the light, I soon learned that I was wrong. She wasn't lonely at all. Veronica and Bruce were sitting on the couch, watching television together. They had their backs to me, and if it hadn't been for the window, I would have been able to smell her hair.

The boxer's ears twitched for a moment, and my muscles froze in response. But it didn't turn around or start barking.

Veronica seemed to be eating dinner, judging by the way she raised her right arm with her elbow pointing out every few seconds. Then she did something that disgusted me, and I almost made the mistake of gasping. She offered some of her food to Bruce and let him eat it from the fork. He licked it off, and I screwed my face up as I noticed his slobber sticking to the fork once she'd pulled it away.

She then ate another mouthful.

My disgust soon changed to indignation. An elegant woman like her had no right to behave in such a disgraceful way. She was breaking the rules of basic human decency. Letting her dog sit next to her on the couch while she ate dinner was one thing, but sharing her meal and her fork with him — no, *it* — was outrageous.

58

I felt like slapping her, and I felt like giving Bruce a hiding. She needed me there beside her, not some filthy mongrel.

I heard a growl. Then, an instant later, Bruce spun around. He snarled at me through the window and gave a warning growl.

By the time he'd started barking, I was off the deck and sprinting back toward my bicycle. I had no idea whether Veronica had seen me.

It wasn't until I was on two wheels and speeding away that the realisation struck me that the first growl I'd heard had been different from the second.

That was the first of many nights spent peering into Veronica's house. Each time I rode up to Bardon, I knew I was sinking deeper into a pit of obsession and anguish from which it would be difficult to climb back out, as indeed it has been and continues to be. Nevertheless, Veronica was under my skin. I pitied and despised and craved this strange and vulnerable woman. I was convinced she needed me. She was lonely and afraid. That's why she was so close to her dog. The animal offered her the companionship and sense of security that a single woman needed, but it wasn't how she ought to live. I had to show her it was me she needed.

Before long, I started sleeping in the park opposite her house and stopped going to work. My memory of this time is unclear, but the more I watched her, the more I wanted her and the more I hated Bruce. I was bitterly jealous of the dog. I became very adept at creeping around in the dark and quickly learned how to avoid being detected. It all came down to paying attention to the direction of the wind, so as to avoid him catching my scent, and to moving in complete silence.

I'd suppressed the last night I watched Veronica from my memory until you dug it up. Of course, I'm glad you did. Otherwise, I would still be roaming the streets like a lost dog and thinking about her. Now, I'm becoming human again.

It was raining heavily that night, but I was impervious to the wet and cold as I crawled out of the reeds growing by the bank of Ithaca Creek and shuffled over to Veronica's house. I forced myself to ignore the bolts of lightning that struck nearby and the crashes of thunder that boomed across the turbulent sky. I steadied my legs and carried on.

I'd fallen into the habit of climbing a jacaranda tree that allowed me a very narrow view of Veronica in the shower. Sometimes, Bruce was in there with her, even though it seemed to be against his will, judging by the way she held him firmly by the collar with one hand while she scrubbed at his body with the other. Naturally, I preferred it when she was alone, but whenever Bruce was with her, I took great pleasure in admiring the way her breasts jiggled as she energetically rubbed soap into his coat.

But that night, the bathroom light was off. I'd evidently missed the show.

There was purple light, not unlike the colour of jacaranda flowers, coming from the room one window down, so I moved a little further along the branch, well aware that I was increasing my chances of slipping, losing my balance, having the branch snap under my weight, or even being struck by lightning. None of that mattered to me at all. I simply had to see her.

The room's white lace curtains were almost closed, and rain was hammering against the window panes, but every now and then, I managed to catch a glimpse of movement. The gap between the curtains exposed the purple lamp whose light fell upon a flat floral-patterned surface behind it.

I realised with delight that I was peering, for the very first time, into Veronica's bedroom.

A flash of lightning lit the sky for a moment and the corresponding boom of thunder made the branch I was perched upon shake. Undeterred, I ventured a little further along, grasping the rough wet surface as firmly as I could.

The movements I'd noticed were ever so slightly clearer now.

After another minute of observation, I noticed that they were rhythmic, like dancing. A moment later, I was able to distinguish a heavenly glimpse of Veronica's white skin through the rain-spattered window. I started breathing heavily, and despite my discomfort, my penis went hard and bulged against the jacaranda branch. There was no doubt about it. She was masturbating. As I watched, I found myself rubbing against the tree in time with her.

After a while, her body arched and she shifted a little toward the head of her bed. It was then that I caught sight of what was on the bed with her.

I felt sick to the core as I realised what was happening. It was disgusting and inhuman. But my shock was cut short by a fork of lightning that ripped through the dark clouds and struck nearby. The last thing I can remember before coming into your care is falling from the branch and hitting the ground as a thunderclap rattled my bones.

Professor Broughton poured another dram of whisky into each glass.

'Remember, Charles, that you promised to keep your lips sealed.'

Charles simply stared at his tutor with an expression of horror and disbelief.

'Are you all right?'

'Yes,' he whispered. 'Well, I suppose so. Tell me, it is true? You're surely playing a joke on me. It's too bizarre to have actually happened.'

Professor Broughton shook his head. 'I'm afraid it's all too real, Charles. Truth is stranger than fiction and all that, right? Now, do remember, you mustn't repeat it to anybody. Your lips are sealed.'

'Repeat it!' Charles said, frowning. 'I don't even want to think about it ever again.'

THE CROWS OF EILDON HILL

My name is Brandon Donovan and I have a burden to share with you, my imaginary listener.

Firstly, let me tell you a little about myself and the three wonderful women in my life. I met my wife, Debbie, at the University of Queensland in 1987. It was the first day of our introductory biology class. Thirty years later, we're more in love than ever and live in a beautifully restored Queenslander on Constitution Road in Windsor. We have two daughters. The elder, Valerie, is now at the University of Queensland too, studying economics, a field that has never appealed to or even appeared comprehensible to me. The younger, Berenice, is in her final year of high school. She wants to follow the family tradition of pursuing tertiary studies, but a number of distractions and obstacles are making that goal more of a challenge than it ought to be. One particular incident that happened recently has interrupted our family's otherwise comfortable existence and cast a dark shadow over Berenice's entire future.

But I'm getting ahead of myself and forgetting that a story must start at the beginning.

Both Debbie and I are biologists. I worked in research for many years before deciding that teaching was what really interested me. There are easier and more financially rewarding ways of earning a crust than teaching a rational scientific field of study to a mob of teenagers in the throes of puberty, but that was what I chose to do. The two or three special youngsters who share your passion are what make it worthwhile. They're the reason you get up in the morning.

Another of my interests, obsessions perhaps, is that of moral philosophy. Many biologists fall into the trap of only seeing the world and the animals that inhabit it as a complex interplay of instinct and environment. I disagree with this view. Humans are animals, strictly speaking, yet we have a number of capacities that differentiate us from the rest of the animal kingdom. Most importantly, we're able to analyse ourselves and our societies. We've developed value systems, and, even if we don't adhere to them, we cannot excuse ourselves from them. Put more simply, we have the capacity, and therefore the duty, to repress instincts that are bestial and uncivilised and can cause harm to ourselves and others of our species. This difference between humans and other animals is why I'm fascinated by the field of moral philosophy.

Of all the animals, crows attract my attention the most. Their language is astonishing. Yes, didn't you know they have a formalised system of vocal communication? I can't claim to be fluent in their tongue, but I'm able to recognise and mimic certain common expressions.

I'm particularly familiar with the crows of Eildon Hill, where I am at this very moment. If you know Windsor, in the north of Brisbane, you'll surely know this landmark. It's a plateau accommodating a water reservoir and mobile phone transmitters. I often jog along the poorly maintained bitumen drive that forms an oval around the reservoir, especially in the minutes before sunrise, just when the crows are at their most active and the air is still quite cool. I don't wake up early for a jog every day. On average, I come up here three times a week. Nobody else is ever around.

Today, my crows are happier than ever. I've given them an exceptional gift.

But it is Berenice who is on my mind, not these birds. I'm worried about her. I've never liked the company she keeps, and she knows it. I had a feeling something like this would happen, but I'd never tell her so. She opened up to her sister; let her heart bleed to her. I overheard her on the phone. I wasn't supposed to know anything about it, and that's the way I want it to stay. They must never know that I know.

It ripped me apart, of course. I almost made the mistake of acting rashly, but I resisted. Instead, I buried my rage and frustration in books. I scoured hundreds upon hundreds of pages for answers. I reread Spinoza, Nietzsche, and Kant, but they left me unsatisfied. Then I decided, or rather remembered, to trust my own judgement. I needed no book to justify what I sensed was right. I decided to follow the necessary course of action, and I promised myself that I would be damned clever about it.

I have been. I'm sure of it.

We've been brainwashed into allowing the law of the land to decide what is right or wrong and into allowing the judicial system to punish those who break it. But this has always seemed insufficient to me, and a man who accepts the dictates of a flawed system is himself guilty of immorality through complacency. Of course, not everybody agrees on what is moral or immoral, or on whether those who have committed evil acts are truly responsible for these acts, or on whether they should be pardoned and given a chance at rehabilitation. Indeed, some even argue that evil doesn't exist at all and that any actions performed by one human with the intention of bringing harm to another result undoubtedly from mental illness beyond the control of the offending individual. Such ideas appear naïve to me. They reek of philosophy based on fear. For many, the idea that evil intent exists in the minds of men and women who are in complete control of their thoughts and actions is too frightening and sinister to believe.

For my part, I don't doubt evil exists. It's in us, and it's as old as we are, if not older. Its origins can be speculated upon, whether we've inherited it from a devil or from instincts that have clung on over the millennia as we've evolved, but its existence is undeniable.

Would you like an example; a personal one? Well, I'm only thinking to myself after all, so my secret will remain safe.

As much as I wish I could forget it, I remember one particular day when I noticed an evil urge in myself. It was terrible, because although I'd always been a good man and knew I would never act in any way that I considered to be immoral, I couldn't ignore the fact that the animal drive to do what my principled mind would never allow was there, lurking like a primitive hunter within my hypothalamus.

It was in summer, about three years ago, and I'd gone up to Coolum for the weekend to stay with some childhood mates in a bungalow by the beach. Debbie and Berenice were visiting Sandra, Debbie's sister, for a couple of days, and Valerie was at home by herself.

Before leaving for the coast, I'd told Valerie that I'd be back around dinner time on Sunday. As it turned out, I'd decided to beat the evening traffic and come back early in the afternoon.

I was tired and thirsty, so the first thing I did when I arrived home was go to the kitchen to get a drink of water. As I poured myself a glass, I looked out the kitchen window and noticed Valerie lying face down by the pool. Her naked body was glistening under the afternoon sun. Even from the kitchen, I could see the pink gash between her thighs. She was hairless. That was what shocked me at first, for some reason. Then what shocked me even more was my reaction.

I grew hard and found myself leaning closer to the window. That rosy opening hypnotised me and filled me with hunger. I felt compelled to go down there.

I had to shake my head to clear my thoughts and jerked my right hand out of my shorts. I hadn't even realised it had slipped down there in the first place.

I felt filthy, so I went straight to the bathroom and took a shower. I forced myself to think of my wife.

That was the day I most clearly understood that we're just animals behind our veneer of civilisation. That said, it also occurred to me that we have the ability, and therefore the moral obligation, to control our instincts and base desires. Those who fail to do this make a conscious decision to be evil.

That's precisely what Jake Warner did the night he raped Berenice at a party and threatened to slit her throat if she ever told anyone. She knew her sister was the only person in the world who would listen to her without insisting she call the police.

There was only one morally acceptable course of action for me to take.

The internet was my first port of call. I typed, *Jake Warner Brisbane*, and spent about fifteen minutes trawling through profiles and database entries that were varied and revealed no pertinent information. I then added, *rapist*, but there were no coherent results. What I did discover was that countless rapists had been found guilty and sentenced to short prison terms only to be released to reoffend. The inefficacy and moral vacuity of the judicial system horrified me.

I kept searching but was unable to find anything that was evidently connected to the monster who had violated my little girl.

What I did next was something I'd always refused to do as a father who respected the privacy of his daughters. But what choice did I have? I snooped around in Berenice's bedroom, using the care of a biologist in the field, determined not to leave any sign of my passage.

I looked at the photographs on her camera. There were numerous from the party that terrible night. I was surprised she hadn't deleted them all, then realised she probably hadn't even picked her camera up since then. There were dozens of faces in those photos, in various stages of drunkenness. I tried to memorise them all.

After that, I scanned her bookshelf and removed copies of her high school yearbooks. After flicking through endless pages of articles on academic prize-winners and some of the most awkward poetry I've ever laid my eyes on, I came to the class photographs. Beneath one was a name that seized my attention with a steely grip.

There it was, in black on white; *Jacob Warner*.

He'd been in his final year in 2011, making him about four years older than Berenice. I studied the black and white picture of him. The quality wasn't very good, but it was a face I recognised immediately from the camera. It was now the face of a young man, not a teenager, but it was the same face, without a shadow of a doubt.

I controlled my excitement and forced myself to place the yearbooks back exactly as I'd found them before returning to the camera. I found the picture of Jake Warner again. He'd photobombed a shot of Berenice and her friends pulling faces and holding bottles of pre-mixed drinks.

I recognised one of those friends. Her name was Nelly and I'd tutored her in biology for a few months until last year. I had to call her about the party, that was clear, but I needed some kind of pretext.

I put the camera back and left the room while I thought about what I could say. Then it hit me. I knew she wasn't interested in biology, so there was no risk. I would call her to tell her I had a friend at the university who was looking for high school students to help with a research project. It was worth a try.

To be honest, while I was dialling her number, I kept telling myself it wasn't going to work. I thought I wouldn't sound casual enough when I asked about the party and who was there, or that she would be in a hurry, as teenage girls seem to always be these days.

But I was wrong. I got enough information to proceed. I learned that a few of the people at the party hadn't been invited, and that two of the gate crashers lived in the very same street. One of them was Jake.

After hanging up, I stared at the phone for what must have been several minutes. I was expecting it to be difficult to know what to do, but it came to me all at once. It was so obvious. I knew what he looked like and in which street he lived. Next, I had to find out exactly where he lived.

I started jogging the length of his street every morning and evening, and it didn't take me long to find the son of a bitch. On the third day, I saw him in a front yard. He was working on a car. I recognised him immediately.

There was a bottle of beer on the ground beside the oily rag upon which his tools lay. It was risky, but this was an opportunity not to be missed. Once he had his back to me, I took the vial from my pocket and walked towards him as quietly as I could. I stooped as I neared the beer bottle and managed to pour the vial's contents into it before he heard me and turned around. By that time, I was standing up straight and had the vial concealed in my hand.

'Can I help you?' he asked, looking me up and down. 'You're not trying to sell anything or convert me, are you?'

I smiled at the monster. It came naturally enough, knowing I'd beaten him.

'Just wondering if you could help me find a café called Treacle. I was told it's around here.'

He wiped his nose with a dirty hand and indicated down the street. 'Turn left at the end of the street and keep going. It's after the roundabout.'

'Thanks,' I said. 'Have a nice afternoon.'

It was going to be his last.

I jogged around the streets for a quarter of an hour before venturing back to the rapist's house. Just as I'd expected, the car bonnet was still up and his tools were still there, but Jake was nowhere to be seen. I looked up and down the street—and confident that my presence hadn't been noticed by neighbours—went into his front yard.

The beer bottle was now empty. Knowing the poison's effect on the body, I was almost certain Jake was slumped dead on the toilet.

A hundred years ago, I could have left it at that. The man's death would have been ruled unusual but of completely natural causes. Nowadays, the substance was detectable, and the risk that a post-mortem would be carried out was too great. I had to dispose of his body thoroughly. There could be no trace of Jake left.

I'll spare you the gory details of how I cut his body into manageable pieces and transported him little by little up here last night, observed only by possums and flying foxes. Suffice to say that now, as the pink glow of dawn tickles the horizon, more crows are arriving by the minute. Never has Eildon Hill been such a hub of avian activity.

I know that nothing but dry bones will remain when night falls.

Black feathered forms caw from the trees, asking my permission to partake in the feast. I reply to them, telling them they're welcome, and they swoop down, thanking me in low rumbling tones. They look at me, staring straight into my core, before sticking their beaks into a thigh or arm and tugging strips of skin and flesh off.

The head has almost been reduced to a skull already. The eyes are always the first morsels to go, followed by the brain, and the soft flesh of the cheeks.

I wonder whether they understand the reason for my gift. It's possible. Crows are very intelligent creatures. They have an encephalisation quotient as high as that of some apes. If they understand, and eat regardless, it means they're willingly helping me. That in turn would suggest they possess a moral fortitude greater than that of most of our species, homo sapiens. This possibility both excites and disturbs me.

The flapping and cawing continues as more crows land near the pieces of Jake.

These winged creatures were regarded as messengers of misfortune in various ancient cultures. Today, we consider ourselves immune to such superstitious beliefs. Yet who can honestly claim not to feel just a little uneasy upon noticing a crow perched on an overhead branch or power line? I can, of course, but can you?

This is all an unfortunate misconception caused by ignorance. Crows are black, highly intelligent, and feast on the dead. These three characteristics provoke irrational fear in us, particularly the last one. However, they're not at all sinister. In fact, they're beneficial to humanity. They thrive on the waste and rot that we so prolifically produce, and help keep our cities clean.

But that's enough of all this idle musing. I mustn't get carried away with my thoughts, telling my tale to myself. Of course, I understand that if I can't stop thinking about crows, it's because I'm trying not to think about Berenice and what she went through. More than once, I've found myself trying to imagine what this abominable man did to her, even to the point of wondering which orifice he penetrated and whether she was left bruised and bleeding. It fills me with rage. Now that he's dead, I almost find myself wishing I'd killed him in a more painful way. But it's too late, and I realise that any form of barbarism would have tarnished the righteousness of my actions.

I ought to go home, just in case the crows attract unwanted attention. Even though we humans tend to ignore bird activity unless it directly affects our busy lives, I need to watch my step. My plan has worked marvellously so far, and I mustn't let my guard down now.

You mustn't think me cold or heartless. This is the first time I've hurt—let alone killed—anyone. Hopefully, it will also be the last. I don't expect to ever forget the terrible things I had to do between the time I found Jake dead on the throne and now. But I'm pleased with myself. By executing this monster, I've prevented him from ever hurting another woman again and have appropriately punished him for what he did to my daughter. Justice has been served, in its purest form.

LAUREN

Lauren was sucking her bottom lip in anticipation as she watched the barman mix her cocktail. It was a ritual for her to get the ball rolling on a Saturday evening with a Lucille at the Bowery, just as it was becoming a ritual for her to only ever pay for that first drink of the night. The barman looked up for an instant and shot her a tantalising smile. He probably recognised her, but she couldn't say for sure. She wondered what he thought of her, if anything at all. The smile had probably meant nothing. She hadn't failed to notice he was generous in that regard. Every half-decent-looking girl got one. There was no reason to read anything into it.

The Bowery was a classy little bar and Lauren always came with the intention of meeting an equally palatable young man. She wasn't interested in drunken bogans or blinged-up wankers, so she never went near the Royal George or the Bank. She didn't go for punks or any other kind of rockers either, so she kept away from the Zoo. Nor were hipsters her thing, so the Alhambra was out of bounds. Apart from the Bowery, the only other bar she frequented was Cloudlands, with its spacious mezzanine and chic jungle atmosphere. It wasn't as intimate as the Bowery though, and its barmen didn't please her as much. The Bowery's fine specimens were enough to make even the most level-headed girl swoon. They were all handsome devils dressed to impress in sleek white shirts, black braces, and smartly cut trousers. Most importantly, they all knew how to mix a killer cocktail.

Just as the barman was putting the finishing touches to his work of art, Lauren noticed a young man slide up beside her. He inserted himself like a coin into a slot between her and a tall blonde who was sipping a Singapore Sling. She twisted towards him and, reaching into her handbag to get her purse, glanced at him for a fraction of a second. They made eye contact.

As brief as it was, the moment was enough to confirm what she'd been hoping. It wasn't the blonde in a red dress so short the lower part of her tanned buttocks were displayed to the public who interested him. Lauren was the one who had caught the attention of this handsome fellow with dark hair, a meticulously groomed moustache, and hungry eyes.

He spoke gently but confidently as his right hand reached out towards the barman with a twenty dollar note.

'I hope you don't mind.'

As a matter of fact, she did. It was more than a little presumptuous of him. He should have offered first. But she didn't refuse, and anyway, the barman hadn't even waited for her permission to accept the payment.

'Thanks,' she whispered.

'I'll have a Scottish Delight,' he told the barman without taking his eyes off Lauren. She wasn't the most beautiful girl in the joint, but she was certainly sexy in an offbeat kind of way, and, more importantly, he felt sure he could manage to end up taking her home with him. He could practically smell the promise on her, as though her flowery perfume was incapable of hiding the less innocent odour her skin was giving off. Despite her elegant green dress and modest make-up, he knew she was nothing but a horny little bitch that would do anything he wanted if he just bought her a few drinks and treated her like a lady for an hour or two. He also knew that she knew that he thought this.

She looked at him in a way that was simultaneously coy and provocative. She wanted to play at being a man-eater, and he was fine with that, but he wondered if she really knew what he was thinking about doing to her.

He studied her tight little body. It was clearly defined by her kinky green dress. He admired her legs without any sense of shame, the way a supermarket shopper might appreciate the allure of a well-packaged rump steak just before picking it off the shelf. They were covered in black stay-up stockings and ended in a pair of shiny green high-heels that seemed to have been tailor-made to match her dress, or was it the other way around?

She wasn't watching him though. Lauren was looking at the hot blonde behind him. She was obviously jealous he'd chosen Lauren over her. An expression of exaggerated surprise covered her heavily made-up face. Lauren winked at her and stuck her bottom lip out in a gesture of mock sympathy. The skank then turned her back and Lauren could have sworn she started pressing her almost bare arse up against him, whatever his name was.

'I'm Lauren. If you're not too busy drooling over my legs, maybe you could have the decency to tell me your name.'

He looked up at her face but, instead of appearing embarrassed, smiled in a way that made her feel moist in her knickers.

'My name's Alex. I'm sorry. I hope you don't think I'm rude. It's just that you're so beautiful, I couldn't help myself.'

Lauren sighed as the barman slid Alex his Scottish Delight. 'You can cut the crap, Alex. I think I liked you better before you opened your mouth. I'm not some dumb blonde bitch who will give you head because you've memorised a book of crappy pick-up lines.'

She wondered if her harsh reaction would make him walk away but was pleased to find that he wasn't going to give up so easily. He just grinned at her as he raised his glass. He found her attitude a massive turn-on.

'Cheers!' The rims of their glasses gently kissed. 'As much as I'm enjoying having that gorgeous creature behind me rub her firm arse against mine, how about we find a spot where we can sit down and talk a little?' he suggested loudly enough for the blonde in question to hear. She promptly turned around and glared at them both.

Lauren laughed. Maybe he was going to be fun after all. She sucked at her Lucille before mouthing 'bye-bye' to the bimbo.

Alex led her towards the back of the narrow bar and sat her down at the only available bench space he could find. He remained standing but leaned forward against the table so he wasn't looming over her.

'So, tell me about yourself, Lauren.' He noticed he could glimpse

73

her milky white thighs peeking out from between the top of her stockings and the hem of her dress. He had the urge to kneel down and lick them.

'What do you want to know?'

'How about, why a girl like you is single?'

She frowned as though his question had disappointed her, and he didn't fail to notice.

'Sorry, well, what colour is your underwear?'

'Try asking a question you probably wouldn't otherwise discover the answer to later tonight.'

He sipped at his drink to hide his grin.

'Let me try again.'

'Make it good, Alex. You were far more attractive when you didn't speak much. Your luck is running out.'

'Ouch!' a nearby male voice said. Alex didn't bother trying to see who had said it.

'Give me a second, okay?'

She looked at him blankly.

'I've got it. What were you doing at exactly three o'clock this afternoon?'

She drained her Lucille dry and looked suggestively at the empty glass. He took it from her but wanted to hear the answer before leaving to get her another drink.

'I was at home, in my bedroom. I was completely naked and studying entomology.'

'Entomology?'

'Yes,' she confirmed. 'You know what that is, don't you?'

'Of course, it's the study of insects. You study insects.'

'Yeah, and I bet that has made your hard on melt.'

He shook his head and went back to the bar without uttering another word. She wasn't just a hot little bitch; she was a brainy one too. That turned him on even more, and, for the record, his erection hadn't wavered since he'd laid eyes on her. His confidence hadn't wavered either, he still felt sure he would take her home with him.

Alex looked around as he waited impatiently for a barman to give

74

him a nod and lend him an ear. He couldn't spot any familiar faces, which was a good thing considering the fact he was in no mood to be interrupted. Lauren was all the company he was interested in having. He didn't always go out alone. He often hit the town with a mate or two. But they had all been a little too busy recently. Luke was usually up for a wild night in the Valley, but Alex hadn't heard a word from him in the last few weeks.

The faces of strangers bobbed up and down around him like buoys in the sea. Several of them were pretty faces belonging to girls Alex would love to take home with him, maybe another night.

When he got back to where Lauren was, carrying a Sazerac in one hand and a Bellini in the other, he was so surprised by what he saw that he almost lost his grip on the cocktails. The blonde in the tiny red dress and Lauren were talking. Well, maybe *talking* wasn't the most accurate way to describe what was happening. They were hissing at each other like cats, and Alex had a feeling it wouldn't be long before the claws came out. He had to do something to calm the situation and, at the same time, show his dominance to both of the females.

'Lauren, who's your friend?' he asked charmingly.

'This jealous bitch isn't my friend.'

'You're a psychopath! I'm not jealous of you.'

'Go away then.'

'Ladies!'

'Fine, I'll go away, but you'd better stop looking at me.'

'I'll look wherever the hell…'

'It's settled then,' Alex interrupted. 'Let's just leave it at that.'

'It's not settled, honey,' the blonde spat. 'She's provoking me!'

Alex looked at Lauren pleadingly. He just wanted the blonde to disappear before the three of them were kicked out of the bar.

'No problem. I'll stop looking at you,' Lauren said. *Bitch*, she thought.

The blonde walked away, and Alex couldn't help but have a quick look at her arse. Her cheeks peeped out from under the hem with each step she took.

'What a bitch!' Lauren whispered. 'What did you get me?'

'A Bellini,' he answered, placing the glass in front of her.

'Excellent choice,' she congratulated him. 'Oh yeah, and thanks for calming us down. You've almost made up for your pathetic questions.'

'As a matter of fact, I've got a few more questions for you. For instance, why do you study naked?'

She rolled her eyes at him, but it was more out of playfulness than mockery.

He just stared at her.

'I was joking,' she eventually answered. 'I was just teasing you. Nobody in their right mind would study naked.'

He smiled at the way she'd thrown the question back at him, trying to make him feel awkward. He didn't bother replying. He just sipped at his Sazerac. The girl was either trying hard to seem up for it or she really was. Surprisingly, he hoped it was the former. It would be a lot more fun that way.

Several cocktails later, they were ready to leave. They were both eager to get to know each other a hell of a lot better in more intimate surroundings.

Lauren went to the ladies' room for what felt like an eternity to Alex. He hoped she wouldn't change her mind while she was there. He knew all too well that women often did that. He didn't know how it happened, but the ladies' room held sway over them, giving them the kind of clarity of mind that often erased all the filthy ideas men had tried to put in their heads. He waited impatiently, checking out some of the other women and wondering if he would get the opportunity to take them home sometime in the future.

When Lauren finally returned, he led her out onto Ann Street. She was as ready and willing as ever.

They stumbled past Downe's Shoes with its dozens of Doc Martens behind the display window and made their way over to the taxi rank opposite the Zoo.

'I'll take you to my place,' Alex said as they waited in the queue.

She tilted her head to one side, and, for a moment, she didn't seem as drunk as he'd thought.

'I would rather we went to mine. After all, I don't really know you.'

Alex tried not to show his disappointment but doubted how successful he was at hiding it. It was a shame. He had a great selection of toys he wanted to use on her. Without them he would be forced to improvise. The only problem was that she wasn't drunk enough.

'Do you have anything to drink at your place?' he asked with an air of innocence.

'Everything you could possibly want.'

They shuffled along until they reached the end of the queue and got into a taxi.

'Where to?' the driver asked.

She gave him her address and he typed it into his GPS before pulling out and driving off along Ann Street, leaving the Bowery, the Brunswick Street Mall with its swarm of drunken night-clubbers, and the much quieter Chinatown Mall behind.

'I still live with my folks,' she admitted with some embarrassment, 'but they're overseas at the moment.'

Alex didn't reply. He just smiled at her and decided he was going to kiss her. It was time to make a move. He wanted to stick his tongue into her mouth and feel its moist warmth. He wanted to taste the cocktails she'd drunk.

She was surprised by his sudden advance but didn't resist as he placed one hand behind her head and pushed her face towards his. The other hand then slipped down between her thighs and a chill ran through him as it edged its way across the thin fabric of her stockings and onto the smooth surface of her skin. He wondered if she would reach down and grab him by the wrist, yanking his hand away. If she did, then it would probably all be over before it had ever really started. But Alex was confident she wouldn't.

It turned out he was right.

They didn't feel ashamed about making out in the taxi. They ignored the driver completely and failed to notice the frown of disgust on his face as he concentrated on his driving and struggled not to glance at them in the rear vision mirror whenever he had to stop at a red light.

Alex sucked at Lauren's lips. They felt like soft alcoholised slugs. Her eyes were closed, but he kept his open. He stared at her eyelids and noticed that she wore a faint shade of green eyeliner. Alex didn't know much about Lauren, but he felt pretty sure he'd guessed what her favourite colour was. For some reason, knowing that personal detail excited him even more. He could feel an enormous pressure building up deep inside. It was begging to be transferred to her.

Lauren opened her eyes. Her lashes brushed against his like startled butterflies. She'd caught him in the act of staring at her. She let out a single breathy laugh and then closed her eyes again. They continued sucking at each other.

Alex's hand crept slowly along the inside of her thigh until the tip of his index finger came into contact with fabric. The urge to slip it under was strong, but he restrained himself and just held his palm pressed against her thigh. Lauren wanted him to touch her there, but, at the same time, she was happy he'd known where to draw the line. This was a man who knew how to play his cards with a perfectly balanced combination of confidence and self-control.

When the taxi eventually came to a halt, the driver had to interrupt them.

'We're here!' he snapped.

Alex looked at the screen to check the fare. $19.10.

He fished a twenty dollar note out his wallet and let the driver keep the change.

Lauren flashed the driver a smile that could only be interpreted as meaning; *I bet you're jealous, aren't you?* Then she slipped out behind Alex.

The taxi disappeared into the night, leaving the pair standing in the darkness of a beautiful Bardon street whose tranquillity contrasted starkly with the noise and lights of the Valley.

Alex looked at Lauren, waiting for her to show him the way. She took him by the hand and led him across the street and up a steep driveway that penetrated a thickly wooded front yard. On either side of them, towering eucalypts whose dry leaves rustled in the gentle breeze were connected to shorter frangipanis and low-growing grevilleas by a wild tangle of jasmine and passion fruit vines. In some places, the vines had even stretched right over the driveway and were clinging to the branches of trees on the other side.

Alex was enchanted. This wasn't a garden; it was a hidden realm of magical beauty. He lived in a share house in West End where there was only just enough room in the front yard for a weed-infested flower bed. Out back was little better with no more than a rusty old Hill's Hoist and a solitary papaya tree. He was suddenly ashamed of his unimpressive and far from intimate home. It was a good thing he'd let Lauren insist on them going back to her place. The atmosphere would be much more conducive to a no-holds-barred liaison, and, more importantly, it was relatively secluded.

He opened his mouth to tell Lauren what he thought of the forest, but she guessed what he was about to say.

'Isn't it just? We used to have a gardener, but we just let it grow now.'

If the front yard was so wildly beautiful, he couldn't begin to imagine how breath-taking it must have been out back. But they were both more interested in spending time indoors.

When they arrived at the front door, Alex realised just how wealthy Lauren's family was. The house was a massive three-storey structure with a verandah around the two upper storeys. The branches of the eucalypts touched the railings of the highest verandah and Alex noticed possums looking down at them from up there. He wondered how many men they had observed her bringing home before. If only he could have asked them.

Lauren inserted the front door key without any difficulty. Alex needed to get her to drink some more. She was nowhere near inebriated enough. He placed a hand on her arse and squeezed, then let his fingers slide up under the hem of her dress.

'Patience,' she whispered. It was the first time she'd tried to slow him down. He ignored her and raised his hand towards her crotch. His fingers touched between her legs. He grinned. It was moist. Yes, he could definitely detect the feel of warm moisture.

A light flashed on and he noticed she was giving him a hard stare. He immediately retracted his hand.

'Alex, you were doing so well.'

The pressure inside him grew even stronger as the terrible possibility that she might want to call it all off struck him. He had to say something to stop that from happening. No! He had to keep his mouth shut and just smile a mock apology.

She started walking up the flight of polished wood stairs. Alex admired the movement of her legs as she climbed, the way her hips swayed from side to side. He wanted to hike her cute little green dress up and tug her panties down so that he could lick her buttocks with all the eagerness of a cat on discovering that somebody had left the butter on the kitchen bench. He resisted the temptation. He just followed her.

She flicked a light on and watched a look of amazement come over Alex's face. It was obvious he hadn't been expecting what he saw. He'd assumed the living room would be minimalist, a rarely used fireplace next to a plasma TV with a coffee table and leather lounge facing. Perhaps there would be a painting or two on the walls, but nothing more. But what he saw was far from that. The living room had dozens of books and scores of empty plates scattered all over it. There were letters all over the floor, some opened and others still sealed, and junk mail lay sprawling here, there, and everywhere. Lauren certainly wasn't a fan of housework.

'I'm sorry. I haven't had time to clean up.' The shame in her voice and guilt on her face made her even sexier.

'That's all right,' Alex shrugged. 'My place is no better.'

'Do you still feel like a drink? I think I've maybe had enough.'

'Oh, come on! Don't let me drink alone. Please. Just have one more with me.' He knew very well that if she agreed to one more, she would end up having several. He looked at her with puppy eyes until she nodded.

'All right, one last drink. What do you want?'

He didn't really mind – something strong – just so long as she would have the same. She needed a spirit that would quickly inebriate her.

'Do you have cognac?'

'Cognac?' she repeated the word as though she'd never even heard it before. 'Let me see.'

She stepped over a ring binder that was packed with more sheets of paper than it was designed to hold and almost tripped on a voluminous tome entitled 'Species Dysphoria' that was dog-eared and bookmarked with sticky notes. Alex marvelled at how serious a student she seemed to be.

After kicking a copy of Brisbane News aside, she knelt down in front of an antique cabinet and turned the tiny key that unlocked it. The doors creaked as she swung them open to reveal two shelves stacked full of all kinds of bottles.

Alex gasped. Her old man certainly appreciated a fine drop. He spotted an almost full bottle of twenty-one year old Bruichladdich, a bottle of Dom Benedictine, two bottles of Fonseca port, and a selection of champagnes and French reds.

'Remy Martin cognac,' she read out loud. 'Is that all right?'

'It certainly is, if your father doesn't mind letting a stranger drink it in his absence.'

'And then having his way with his daughter,' she added cheekily. 'Don't worry. He won't even notice.'

'Are you sure?' he asked, referring to the cognac.

'Yeah, I'm sure. What do you care anyway? I don't think either of us is on the hunt for a long-term meet-the-parents sort of relationship, or have I got you all wrong?'

'You're one hell of a girl. No, you haven't got me wrong.'

'I didn't think so.' She removed the bottle along with two champagne flutes.

'Have you never tried cognac?'

'No,' she admitted, shaking her head.

'Have some with me then, won't you?'

She looked at him, and he could see she didn't feel entirely comfortable with the idea. For the first time since they had met, she'd allowed a seed of suspicion to germinate in her mind.

'It's one of the finest brandies in the world. You shouldn't drink it out of a champagne flute though.'

'What should you drink it out of?'

'A balloon snifter.'

'Excuse me?'

'May I?' He nodded towards the cabinet.

'Make yourself at home. You're the man of the house tonight.'

He smiled as he stepped over to the liquor cabinet and knelt down. *Man of the house.* He liked the sound of that. Hidden in a corner behind the wine and whisky glasses were two snifters. It was obvious they were seldom put to use. He pulled them out and had to blow a few specks of dust off them.

As he stood up, Lauren handed him the bottle of Remy Martin and asked, 'Will you do the honours while I put some music on?'

He nodded obligingly and set the bottle and glasses down on the coffee table. He then sat down on the lounge and watched Lauren as she switched two lamps on, turned the ceiling light off, and then slotted her iPhone onto its dock. She moved so deliberately, as though each movement was being carried out in order, like a ritual. Alex thought about the possums again. How many men had they seen step through those front doors? He could tell she wasn't unfamiliar with setting up a romantic atmosphere. She'd gone through those motions many times before.

A pang of jealousy started to gnaw at Alex, but he succeeded in nipping it in the bud. He pushed it out of his mind. What did that matter to him? Neither of them was innocent. They had both agreed to spend the night together for one reason alone – carnal satisfaction – even though neither of them could really pretend to know what the other's concept of that pleasure might be.

Lauren put some strange music on. It sounded like the forest with its subtle string instruments and a rustling sound that reminded him of the eucalypts outside. It was a little creepy, and it certainly wasn't the kind of music that usually turned him on, but if it made her more relaxed and got her to drink up, he could put up with it.

He poured the cognac, filling the glasses to the rim. The splashing sound of the precious brandy and the way it glimmered warmly in the soft light was somehow deeply erotic. He looked up at Lauren again as she turned around. He noticed the momentary look of concern on her face as she saw how much cognac he'd poured, but she hid it well and he pretended to be unaware of it. He smiled at her and she relaxed. She walked over and sat down beside him.

Alex handed her a glass and they touched rims. The high note of glass on glass matched the mystical music perfectly. Alex watched her lips through the bottom of her snifter as she took a cautious sip of cognac. A tiny amount of the amber liquid flowed into her mouth. She lowered the glass and swallowed before parting her lips to release a breath of potent air. Then she sucked at her bottom lip.

'What do you think?'

'I love it.'

She took another sip, longer this time.

'Be careful, it's a strong drink for a girl like you.'

'Is that right?' she answered with defiance.

He just nodded and watched her drain the glass dry. She opened her mouth and stuck her tongue out so he could see she'd finished it all. He felt himself growing even harder, the urgent need to explode coming back. But it was much too early for that.

'Do you want a little more?'

'Sure, but finish yours first.'

He drained his glass. They would have to be careful. If they drank too much too quickly, they would end up falling asleep. He poured another glass each, but instead of handing hers back, he left it on the coffee table and pulled her towards him. He kissed her quickly on the mouth and then started sucking at her neck. She responded by running her hand down his torso until her fingers reached the button of his trousers. She fumbled at it, and he wanted to laugh at her clumsiness but managed to hold it in. He slid his hand under her dress and rubbed between her legs. He wasn't hesitating any longer. His fingers crawled under the moist fabric of her knickers and explored her perfectly smooth folds of skin. He let out a satisfied groan and rubbed slowly. His fingers stuck together as though he'd touched spilt honey.

She managed to get his button undone and tugged his fly open, then her hand slipped inside his trousers and started caressing him.

All of a sudden, something made a dull thud outside. The sound startled Alex and made him look up from Lauren's neck. He glanced over the back of the couch in the direction of the wide sliding doors that separated the interior of the house from the verandah and the small but dense forest beyond. Even though the lighting in the living room was low, it was enough to make the glass doors act as a mirror. He saw a shadowy imitation of himself looking back towards the couch.

'Don't worry,' Lauren whispered in his ear as she gently stroked him. 'It's just possums.'

'Oh, of course, there must be dozens of them in those trees.'

The glass doors didn't give the impression of providing much security. He wondered whether Lauren was afraid of being home alone at night. It wouldn't be difficult for a burglar or rapist to break in.

Alex picked his glass of cognac up and took a sip. Lauren followed his lead. No, she wasn't worried about burglars. A girl who invited a complete stranger back home didn't let such possibilities bother her.

There was another thud, followed by a scratching sound. Alex looked towards the glass doors again and caught a glimpse of movement obscured by the reflection of one of the lamps.

He turned back to Lauren. She was unconcerned, still sipping at her cognac. She was right, of course; it was nothing more than possums carrying out their nocturnal shenanigans.

Alex waited for her to put her glass down. It was already almost empty. He gazed into her eyes, making a silent request, and somehow she understood. She picked her glass up again and drained it, licking the rim to make sure she hadn't wasted a drop. He

84

finished his off too. Then Lauren stood up and walked towards a corridor on the far side of the room. She was starting to think the cognac might have been stronger than she'd anticipated. Alex had warned her, but she'd shrugged him off, wanting to pretend she could handle her drink. Now she was stumbling in a way she knew wasn't very attractive, but despite her efforts, she couldn't control herself. She hoped she wasn't making Alex regret coming back with her. She hoped she wasn't so drunk she wouldn't be able to enjoy the occasion.

It was so dark in the corridor that Alex barely noticed her awkward gait. He was feeling a little drunk too and had to concentrate on where he was going in a house that he didn't know at all. When he felt the doorframe and nothing after it, he assumed he was in her bedroom. He waited for her to find the light switch, but it seemed to take a long time. He was beginning to suspect that she intended to make love in the dark. That would be out of the question; he was a diner who liked to see what he was eating.

Then a dim light came on and lit her bed up like a delicate mediaeval tapestry. He breathed a sigh of relief.

Her hand took his and she led him towards the bed. She pushed him down on it with the kind of force that meant she was going to run the show. He decided to play along for a while.

'Just watch,' she said.

He nodded.

Lauren started dancing, or rather swaying from side to side in what was supposed to be the opening of a striptease. She looked ridiculous, but that didn't matter at all, because Alex wasn't interested in the striptease one little bit. He was just biding his time.

She pulled her green dress up over her head and almost lost her balance trying to get it off. Her arms were trapped.

Alex almost laughed at her. He didn't get up to help, not because he didn't want to risk offending her, but because he was getting a kick out of her predicament. At that moment, she was sexier than she'd been all night, standing there in her stay-up stockings and almost transparent black knickers and bra with her sleek green dress wrapped around her head.

Try asking a question you probably wouldn't otherwise discover the answer to later tonight. That's what she'd said when he asked the colour of her underwear. She'd been acting like a femme fatale at the Bowery, a far cry from the ravishingly silly spectacle now squirming in front of him like a worm on a hook.

Alex didn't help her, but he wasn't going to just sit there and watch her either. He could tell that it was going to take her a while to work her way free and that now was his chance to make a move. He slipped off the bed and crept back into the dark corridor. His destination was the kitchen. He wanted to see what she had in the fridge.

It only took him a minute to find what he wanted, and once he'd returned, holding it behind his back, she'd just about managed to get a grip of her dress again.

'Do you want a hand?'

'No, it's all right. Sorry.'

He got back onto the bed as she pulled the dress free and tossed it theatrically into a dark corner of the room as though her difficulty had never even happened. She placed her hands on her abdomen and ran them up towards her bra before cupping her breasts and then starting to dance awkwardly again. Alex had seen a few stripteases in his time and this was one of the most pathetic, but, for some reason, that made it all the more enjoyable. He reached into his trousers and started stroking himself, half expecting her to tell him to stop. But she didn't. She smiled broadly. So, he kept doing it.

Lauren moved closer to the foot of the bed. She placed the index finger and thumb of each hand on the top hem of her knickers. Her other fingers stuck out like tail feathers. Swaying her hips from side to side, she slipped her panties down ever so slowly, until they had gone past her knees and dropped the rest of the way all by themselves. Even though the light was behind her and directed towards the bed, he could make out her immaculately waxed lips. They were pouting, hungry for a warm kiss.

Alex pulled his trousers down a little so she could watch him

86

stroking himself.

She crawled onto the bed and removed her bra before edging even closer to him, lowering her head. A chill of excitement ran through his groin as her cognac soaked tongue lapped at his testicles. Then it licked up his shaft and curled around the head. She slid her mouth over him, and he reached down and stimulated her nipples for a while before moving his hands up onto her back and towards her head. He combed her hair tenderly with his fingers for a minute but then started to push down on her head until he was almost entirely inside her. She tried to pull back up, but he didn't let her at first, and, when he did, she gasped for breath and almost vomited on him.

She slapped him hard, got up on her knees, shuffled over him, and sat on his face, smothering him. It was supposed to be his punishment, and she wanted to know whether he would accept it or resist.

He tilted his head back so he could breathe and began licking her hungrily. She decided to forgive him for the way he'd treated her and reached down and pleasured him manually at the same time.

Their bodies tingled with growing pleasure until Alex could tell that Lauren was about to come. He stopped licking and lifted her gently off him, then lay her down on the bed. He ignored her groan of complaint and pulled a zucchini out from under a pillow.

'What the hell!' she roared.

'What's wrong?' he asked calmly, pretending it was a normal part of any sexual encounter. 'It's no big deal.'

'Are you fucking nuts? Where did you get that? My fridge! You got that from my fridge?'

'Hey, just relax,' he whispered.

'No way! You're out of your mind!'

'Oh, come on. It's just a bit of fun.'

Lauren looked scared out of her wits. She just stared at the zucchini as though she'd never seen one before in her life. It was the first time she'd ever contemplated a vegetable being used in such a way.

She looked up at Alex. God, he was handsome, and so desperately excited!

She frowned as she said, 'All right. But you have to let me try something afterwards.'

'Whatever you want,' he agreed smugly.

Lauren rolled reluctantly onto her back and parted her knees.

'Gently!' she warned him.

It hadn't been so bad after all. She hadn't climaxed like that in a long time.

Now it was her turn.

She walked off towards a dark corner of the room until her perfect white buttocks bending over were all Alex could see. He heard a drawer being opened and something clinked as it was removed.

'Cuffs?'

She stepped back towards him, smiling sweetly.

He touched himself. He was still hard.

'Be patient,' she told him. 'I'll take care of that. Just put your hands behind your head.'

He was only too happy to obey.

Lauren snapped the cuffs into place and checked that they were secure, then she picked the zucchini up and held it menacingly in front of him.

Alex gulped nervously and shook his head.

She laughed. 'Don't worry. That's not what I'm into.'

'What are you into then?'

She smiled, but it wasn't so sweet now.

He shuddered and felt himself go limp. She wasn't the same girl she'd been a moment ago.

'What are you into?' he asked again. There was a nervous edge to his voice this time.

Lauren walked over to the door, and, for a minute, he thought she was going to leave him there. But she stopped at the doorway and flicked a switch.

Light flooded the room, exposing every corner of it and illuminating its strange features. Glass vivariums containing branches and greenery lined the walls on either side, making it look like they were in the middle of a jungle.

'I got the idea from Cloudlands,' she told him. There was a crazy glint in her eye.

'What idea?'

'The idea of turning my room into a habitat for insects,' she replied slowly, as though it should have been immediately obvious to him.

'Oh, of course. You study entomology. I almost forgot.'

'Almost forgot?' she snarled. 'Let's be honest for a change, Alex. You never really cared, did you?'

He tried to speak, but his chin was shaking.

'You just wanted to use me for your base desires. I'm nothing more than a sexual object for you to play with. You just wanted to make me feel cheap. I'm just a slut. That's all I am. I hang out in bars waiting for some creep to buy me drinks and have his way with me.'

'No,' he stuttered. 'I thought you were into it.'

'I am, of course,' she smiled sympathetically. 'You were just following your instincts. I know all about that. All animals have them, and people are no exception. I have instincts too. It's just that mine are a bit messed up.'

'What do you mean?' Alex managed to ask.

'Just look around.'

He looked at the vivariums but couldn't see what was in them other than greenery.

She answered his unspoken question.

'Praying mantises.'

He shuddered instinctively.

'That's right. I'm a praying mantis.'

Alex said nothing. He suddenly remembered the title of the textbook that had been lying on the living room floor, alongside an overloaded ring binder; *Species Dysphoria*. He hadn't given it much thought at the time, because the branch of biology that had been on his mind had been of a far more practical nature, but he now suspected he knew what the title meant.

'Do you know what they do after mating?' she asked him.

He did, of course, but didn't dare answer.

'Look up there.'

He followed her gaze and found himself wanting to scream. But he couldn't.

A shelf stretched across the wall above the bedroom door. On it were five large glass bottles filled with some kind of clear liquid. The first contained the severed head of a middle-aged man with greying hair and intelligent features.

'Daddy,' she explained. 'He couldn't help himself. I guess you could even say he lost his head over me.'

She looked to see if Alex was laughing, but his features were frozen in a grotesque mask that was transfixed by the row of glass receptacles.

'Even great human intellects are built on a foundation of instinct. We're all just animals, Alex. Humans think they're better than all the others. They even believe that mammals are superior to reptiles and birds. Insects? Well, they're considered no more than a mere nuisance. But I know better. *Insecta* is the most enduring class. It has survived the trials and tribulations of the ages and even now rules the world. Humans are nothing without insects. Their instincts have a far greater impact on the world than all our knowledge and inefficient industry. The praying mantis is one of the finest creatures on the face of this planet, Alex. Humans don't deserve to be arrogant. They're pathetic compared to mantises. They should aspire to be more like them...'

But Alex wasn't listening to her rant. He was just staring at the shelf. The second and third bottles held the heads of two young men, and he realised with horror that, despite its condition, he recognised one of them.

'Luke!' he managed to gasp. 'You psychotic bitch!'

'Oh, you knew him? Well, if it's any consolation, he didn't give me as much pleasure as you did. None of them were up to your standard.' There was no remorse in her voice; not even a hint of guilt. There was nothing that remotely resembled human emotion. There had only been a slight lifting of the eyebrows upon hearing Luke's name; a fleeting admission of authentic surprise.

It had all been an act. She felt nothing for him. If his mind hadn't been so thoroughly soaked with terror, it would have been drowning in the realisation that he'd meant nothing to her, perhaps even less than she'd meant to him. He'd simply been used for sexual stimulation. He'd been an essential component in a preordained mating ritual.

But Alex wasn't looking at Lauren, and his mind was in no state to attempt the futile task of trying to comprehend what precisely was wrong with her and what kind of expert help she would need to address her case of dysphoria. His gaze was fixed on the shelf, and he didn't fail to notice that the fourth and fifth bottles were empty.

They were so invitingly empty. It almost felt as though the bottles were actually *calling* him.

He still wanted to scream, but he could barely even draw a breath.

Lauren dropped slowly, instinctively, to her knees and reached under the bed for a toy that was far more terrifying than any mere vegetable.

The helpless human male didn't even notice what the naked mantis girl was pulling out until it was too late for his stunned mind and bound hands to even make an attempt at resistance. She moved with tremendous speed, leaping onto the bed, and by the time she was on top of him, straddling his slumped body, his head had bounced off the mattress and struck the floor with a beastly thud.

MILK

Chelsea Bishop was obsessed with getting her impeccably manicured hands on whatever money could buy. A simple but clever balancing act of sucking up and backstabbing, refined over the years, was the key to her success. The tactical application of her skills had enabled her to seduce and marry Christopher Bishop, the wealthiest man in her expansive circle of friends, and also guaranteed that she never failed to get what she wanted in her professional life.

While many women in her superannuation firm wasted their time complaining about the glass ceiling, Chelsea was riding the lift all the way to the top floor. So far, it hadn't really been all that difficult either. She'd dug up enough dirt on more promising colleagues to ruin their careers while carefully safeguarding her own reputation and lining herself up for promotion after promotion.

For the granddaughter of penniless Polish immigrants, she'd done extraordinarily well. She was living the highlife in a Hamilton hilltop mansion and she got a perverse pleasure out of driving her gleaming white Audi Q7 4x4 as aggressively as possible. Her home loomed high above Kingsford Smith Drive and the Brisbane River, taunting the lesser elitists below. Her vehicle had been chosen to complement the residence. It was a rolling reminder to others of just how prosperous she'd become.

But of all the challenges Chelsea had faced to date, motherhood was going to be the most trying. Instead of mollifying her competitive nature, it provided her with yet another weapon with which to wage war. She felt compelled to make sure that her baby would be better off than anybody else's, and she was spending as much money as required to complete the mission. She could afford just about everything she wanted for him; everything, that is, except for one very precious commodity.

Chelsea was convinced that formula was inferior to breast milk, and so that was that as far as she was concerned. Breast milk was all that would be fed to her little George. The problem was that he had a phenomenal appetite. He would suck her dry and then cry until he went red. He was never satisfied.

Her doctor thought she was exaggerating, quite simply because what she described was unheard of. All he did was assure her that the infant was getting all the nutrition required and point out that the fact he was putting on weight was obvious enough. He told her to either put up with it or switch to formula milk. Her reply was to inform him that the Bishop family would be changing doctors.

Chelsea sought to distract George in all sorts of ways. She played soothing music after feeding. She took him for strolls in his Aston Martin Silver Cross pram. But nothing worked for more than a few minutes. The urge for milk was always there.

She forced herself to endure his insatiability day in and day out for the first two weeks of his life but told Christopher that it simply couldn't go on. It was torture. It wasn't the child's fault, of course, but it was unbearable all the same.

'You've got to do something, Christopher. There has to be a solution!' she practically shouted at him one night.

It was three o'clock in the morning and the pair had been woken up yet again by an ear-piercing wail.

He drew a deep breath and thought about how to answer his distraught wife in a way that would prevent her from getting as agitated as George was. But the solicitor's sharp brain wasn't at its prime at such an ungodly hour.

'There's no other solution. You'll have to follow the doctor's advice and supplement his diet with formula.'

'My baby will not consume formula! What an irresponsible thing to say!'

'Well, what do you want me to say?' he pleaded. *It's not my fault your tits can't produce enough milk for our son*, he thought.

'You have to get him more breast milk,' Chelsea mused as she got out of bed and went over to George's cot. She could tell there was some milk in her breasts but doubted it would be enough.

'Get him more breast milk? How do you expect me to do that?' he asked.

'Forget it! Just go back to sleep!' she snapped, holding George to her left breast. His little mouth was agape, and when he felt her sore nipple brush his lips, he lunged for it.

Chelsea winced as the toothless piranha started sucking.

'I'm going to lie down in the living room,' Christopher said.

'Go on then! Flee the torture chamber!'

He hurried out, muttering under his breath, and stopped in the kitchen to pour himself a glass of water.

As he sipped, looking through the window at clouds teasing the softly glowing surface of the moon, a thought occurred to him. Maybe it was the pale colour of the celestial orb that had given him the idea, or perhaps it was its perfect roundness. It was difficult to say. The idea was without a doubt the strangest he'd ever had, but he was confident he could pull it off. After all, money was no object.

Christopher placed the glass in the sink and continued towards the living room, where darkness and the ticking of a clock enveloped him completely. He stretched himself out on the lounge as best he could, and while he waited for sleep to come, knowing it would not come easily that night, he worked out the details of his plan.

He woke up with a stiff neck but a clear head. Christopher Bishop never needed to jot notes down. He had an excellent memory, even when he was tired or distracted. As he made himself a coffee, he ran the plan through his mind and was satisfied that even in the cold light of morning, it still seemed completely plausible, despite its absurdity.

Coffee in hand, he crept into the bedroom and found Chelsea and George sleeping soundly. She was lying on her back with the bedspread tangled like seaweed across her waist. Her pink and red striped nightie hung open and her breasts were splayed out. George

94

was curled up between them like a leech at bursting point. Even in his sleep, his rosy lips, which were barely visible between his fat cheeks, rested on one of his mother's bloated and cracked nipples. They were both exhausted. They needed him to provide for them, and quickly.

As soon as he'd finished his coffee and got dressed, Christopher jumped into his golden chariot, a BMW X5, and punched a number into his mobile phone as he drove out of his garage.

'Steve, how are things out your way?... Good to hear... So, the council is still in the dark about all that?... That's great!... Actually, that's the reason I'm calling... George has got one hell of an appetite. He simply can't get enough milk... You can say that again! It will be a long time before I get anywhere near Chelsea's tits again, especially if I can't solve this problem... Yeah, I think I can, as a matter of fact. I know this is going to sound strange, but we've both made successes out of some less than conventional ideas before, haven't we?... This one is even weirder, light years weirder... Listen. I'll tell you what I want, and you just let me know whether it's feasible, what it would cost, and whether you want in, all right?... Good.'

'Good evening, sweetheart,' Christopher called charmingly as he stepped into the house. But when Chelsea leaped into view at the end of the hallway and scowled at him, he realised that his attempt at cajoling his wife was futile.

'Shhh!' she hissed at him like a threatened snake as she rushed forwards. 'I've just put George to sleep. Don't come barging in like that!'

Christopher kept his lips sealed, even though he was begging to tell the bitch he was just trying to be nice, that he wanted nothing more than to get the evening started on the right foot. Instead, he said, 'Sorry. I'm going to grab myself a beer and drink it quietly on the back deck.'

He closed the door gently and started off along the hallway.

'Hold on second,' Chelsea whispered urgently. 'Aren't you forgetting to tell me something?'

'Just give me a couple of minutes to take a leak and get a brew from the fridge, and then I'll tell you all about it, all right?'

Chelsea nodded excitedly.

'Try to calm down a little.'

He regretted his words instantly. But there was no need. Chelsea had taken it well. She nodded again, more slowly now, and went out to the deck.

Christopher joined her about three minutes later. The instant he'd knocked the top off a bottle of Mountain Goat ale, she asked him again, 'So, what's your solution?'

'It will take a couple of days to get into full flow, but once it does, life is going to be a lot easier for us,' he began.

'Yes, yes. I can hold off for a couple of days at most. Come on. Tell me about it.'

So, he told her. He explained the plan in detail, and as he spoke, he watched her reaction. At first, her eyes widened and her jaw dropped, the sheer lunacy of his idea demanded such a reception. But Chelsea held her tongue, which was no mean feat for her, as he continued. The planning was remarkable. She had to admit that. Before long, her eyes narrowed mischievously and her mouth closed. Shock morphed to smug contentedness.

Christian knew she was already sold before he asked, 'What do you think about that then?'

She squeezed her knees tightly together for a second, and Christian could have sworn he noticed her shiver ever so slightly, despite the warmth of that typical Brisbane day.

'Come on,' she said, biting her lip and taking him by the hand. 'Put your beer back in the fridge. You can finish it later.'

He hadn't expected the news to have quite *that* effect on her.

As she led him towards their bedroom, he decided that he would keep all the frustration he felt towards her bottled up inside a little longer, just until the right moment when the pressure would be so great he'd have to unleash it all.

Annie Darrow wasn't used to getting calls to the landline phone. All of her friends and family got in touch with her on the mobile. Whenever the landline rang, she hesitated to answer, not knowing who it might be. Already that morning, she'd ignored two calls to her mobile from Darren, her ex-partner who now lived on the other side of town. Maybe he was trying to trick her into talking to him by calling the landline. He knew she was doing it tough on government benefits, and every now and then, when he needed a fuck and none of his other slags were available, he would try to seduce Annie by rocking up to the house with plastic bags full of shopping or a new pair of panties or pyjamas for her. He no longer tried to win her over with ice. Although it had taken him a while to really believe it, he now accepted that she'd given drugs the boot once and for all. Having her third child, Shelly, had convinced her to go clean. If only Shelly's father would contact her. He wasn't too bad as men went. But Annie knew he wouldn't. Unlike her eldest child's dickhead of a dad, he'd moved on to greener pastures, and perkier young tits.

'What the fuck do you want?' she asked the telephone as she got up from the plastic chair she always sat in when feeding. Her voice, despite the vulgarities it ushered and the weariness it portrayed, still held a hint of the sweet young girl it had once belonged to.

The phone rang out before Annie could get to it and little Shelly cried with outrage at having been ripped away from the nipple of her mother's swollen left breast. Annie shushed her and rocked her back and forth.

'Don't worry, Shelly honey,' she whispered. 'Probably some fucking arsehole of a curry muncher trying to scam us.' Annie's mangled nipple squirted milk into the baby's eyes as she grabbed her tit and shoved it back into the searching mouth.

When the phone rang again, some time later, little Shelly was having a nap, so Annie rushed to answer it before it woke her daughter up.

'Hello.'

Annie frowned as she listened to the voice at the other end.

'No, I can't work. I'm a full-time mum. I've got three kids. That's hard work, you know?'

Her frown softened. 'Good. I'm glad you realise that. Most people don't.'

She nodded patiently.

'I'm listening.'

Her eyes widened with disbelief. 'Say again. How much?'

She put her free hand over her mouth and almost gasped, but decided she needed to play it cool.

'What kind of job is this?' she asked suspiciously.

Her face screwed up as she listened.

'You're having me on, aren't you?'

It was weird work but an easy way to make some cash, and serious cash too.

'I don't know. That's a bit strange, and I'm not sure it's even legal,' she said, hoping to push the pay up even higher.

She drew a sharp breath, not happy with what she was hearing.

'What do you mean I've already done illegal work before? Who says so?'

She bit her lip.

'Yeah, yeah, all right then. Yes, I accept the terms.'

She smiled to herself.

'No, I'm not.'

'You can do a blood test if you like. I'm clean.'

'No problem. I know a few others. How many more do you need?'

'Do you want me to call them for you?'

She nodded excitedly.

'Three hundred per name and number? Sure, that sounds reasonable,' she said as calmly as possible. 'Call me back in fifteen minutes.'

She hung up and put her hands over her face, rubbing it as though to make sure she was awake. The whole conversation had been like a strange dream; the kind she'd often had back when she was still using. A peculiar feeling flooded through her tired body, reminding her of the local creek during storm season. She felt privileged and lucky, but at the same time, so very cheap and dirty.

Annie usually downed at least two cups of strong black coffee for breakfast, but the man on the phone had insisted she wasn't to consume any caffeine that morning. She drank a glass of orange juice instead.

Once she was ready, she checked the address of the dairy farm again and grabbed the car keys. It was still dark outside and she was barely awake, but it was only a twenty-minute drive along quiet country roads.

Her rusty Barina rattled as she drove over potholes her headlights struggled to find in the gloom. Shelly had whinged a little at first but was soon fast asleep.

The sun was licking the horizon as she arrived. A dozen other rusty bombs were parked in front of the plain-looking milking shed. She recognised several of them. The white Fiesta with a dent in the driver's side door belonged to Margie, who needed to make money by any means necessary in order to stay afloat and keep well away from Dazza and his nasty temper. Sal's Corolla was there too. Annie was surprised the pile of crap was still rolling.

Shelly woke up and started wailing as Annie brought her car to a halt.

'Take it easy, sweetie. Mummy's got some work to do.'

Her pleading only annoyed the infant even more.

Then, as Annie switched the headlights off and cut the motor, a figure appeared from the door to the shed and walked over to her.

She got out of the car and unbuckled her daughter from the baby seat in the back.

'Morning.'

'Hello,' Annie replied unenthusiastically.

The man had a bushy brown beard that covered his red and grey chequered shirt. He looked Annie up and down and grinned as his glanced at her ample cleavage.

'The wife'll look after ya littl'un,' he informed her, waving a sandpapery hand towards a plump woman who had appeared out of thin air. 'She'll take 'er up to the house and look after 'er. You can go to the loo if ya want, and then pop back down 'ere.'

'I'm fine,' Annie replied.

She didn't want to leave Shelly alone but had no choice. There was work to be done and money to be had. She handed her daughter to the farmer's wife and she ceased complaining immediately.

Annie was both relieved and surprised.

'Got a way with young'uns, my girl.' The woman's jowls wobbled as she spoke. 'I've 'ad six o' me own.'

Annie nodded.

'You ready?' the farmer asked.

'Yeah,' Annie said, but didn't sound too sure of herself.

'You was told the nature o' the job?'

'I was.'

He grinned.

'You must be making a buck or two out of this deal,' she mused. 'Who's it all for?'

'That's none of ya beeswax!' he snapped. 'You and me both are 'ere to do a job and keep our traps shut 'bout it. Understand?'

'Yeah, sure.'

'Follow me then.'

The farmer led Annie to the entrance to the shed. She could hear the humming of machinery and the chatting of women. There wasn't a cow to be seen or heard.

As she entered, Annie's mouth gaped and her nipples hardened. She'd been told what to expect but was still shocked to see it.

Somebody out there, somebody with serious cash, needed a lot of human breast milk.

'Hi, Annie!' several of the women called over the drone of machinery. Others, strangers, just glanced at her briefly and continued chatting loudly together.

There were more than twenty women in the shed, all bare-breasted and hooked up to the milking machines like dairy cattle. Each nipple had a teat cup attached to it.

Annie felt humiliated.

She wanted to cry.

She wanted to run out of the shed, grab Shelly, and race back home.

'Sit 'ere,' the farmer told her, and she found herself obeying him, taking her place between two strangers.

They both looked happy, and Annie found herself thinking that maybe, once the cups were attached and the milk flowing, it would all be just fine – almost natural.

'Get ya tits out,' he instructed, staring at her chest.

She took her cardigan and top off. She wasn't wearing a bra. There had been no point in putting one on.

Her nipples were already erect and leaking.

The farmer took a teat cup with his right hand and grabbed a breast with his left. His palm and fingers were rough, and Annie only just managed to resist the urge to slap him.

'Ouch!' she cried as he attached the first cup. It hurt like all buggery.

The women beside her giggled.

'What's wrong with you freaks?' she hissed at them.

The farmer took her other breast and pushed the nipple into the second cup. The pain was sharp, like needles.

Annie was crying, but she kept thinking about the cash. She needed it.

The cups throbbed at her nipples, tugging at them, inducing the flow of milk. It didn't take long before the pain subsided and she started to relax.

The women to either side of her smiled knowingly.

'It's not so bad after a few minutes,' the one on her right told her. 'Just forget your self-respect for a while and think about the money.'

'It's our little secret,' the other woman added.

Annie looked down at her nipples pulsing inside the teat cups. Her liquid gold was squirting into the receptacles and flowing along tubes towards a central cistern.

The women were all the same. There were dozens of breasts being emptied. She told herself not to be ashamed or to feel cheap. After all, they were just doing a day's work like everybody else. It was a case of supply and demand, or whatever it was called. She had milk to give and some rich bitch whose boobs obviously didn't work had money to spend on it.

She decided to take the advice of the woman on her right. She closed her eyes and thought about the money.

HORROR AT HOLLOW HEAD

It was a Tuesday morning and Hollow Head was dead quiet. The locals were still resting from the excitement of the weekend, when city folk would swarm like ants to a picnic. Seagulls glided past the red and white lighthouse that stood atop the headland after which the town was named. Sheoaks and pandanus trees, twisted by the unrelenting might of the sea wind, grovelled around it.

To the east of the lighthouse was a sheer cliff. To the west was the unoccupied keeper's house that served as a toilet block and housed a confectionary vending machine. A narrow road led down the steep inland slope to an intersection where the old coastal road, full of potholes and grooves, became the well-maintained esplanade.

There were just three old houses and the maritime museum along the esplanade before *Bygone Books and Maps* marked the start of the commercial stretch.

A little brass bell sounded as Kevin Granger opened the door and stepped inside, followed by Neil. They were both tall men with tanned complexions. Their deep-set hazel eyes, large ears, and receding hairlines were so remarkably similar. Everybody they met took them to be brothers, much to Kevin's pleasure. He hadn't planned on fatherhood at eighteen, but it had happened, and it had changed him. The lost and irresponsible adolescent had grown up quickly, and he'd handled parenthood reasonably well, in his own opinion. Much better than Neil's mother, at any rate. Now, twenty-five years later, they were as close as any father and son could be, and they were quite successful at their unusual, and not entirely legal, jobs.

The counter was cluttered with brochures, bookmarks, and correspondence, but there was nobody behind it.

Kevin looked around the shop. There were precariously leaning stacks of books everywhere, towering up from the floor and packed carelessly onto shelves that looked as though they might collapse at any moment.

Neil studied the shelves behind the counter. That was where the owners of places like this tended to keep the really interesting wares. But there were just photographs, mostly black and white pictures of fishermen wearing flat caps and smoking pipes. In the middle of the top shelf, the largest of the photographs was in colour. It was a simple portrait of a young woman with a long face and short, hooked nose. Above it, a laminated sheet of paper was stuck to the wall. It bore two words: *In memoriam*.

'Neil. Have a look at this.'

'Where are you, dad?'

Kevin popped up from behind one of the shelves and waved a dusty hardcover in the air. As he did so, something slipped from within it and landed between two stacks of boating magazines. He peered into the gap and tried to fish whatever it was out. After several attempts, he succeeded in doing so without sending the stacks of books crashing to the floor.

'What does it say?' Neil asked before Kevin even had a chance to unfold the yellowed paper.

'Give us a second.'

He opened it. A smile immediately crept onto his face.

'It's a map of Hollow Head, and it looks bloody old.'

'Any use to us?'

'Maybe,' Kevin whispered as he slipped the paper into his pocket.

'What's the book about?'

Kevin turned the cover so his son could read it. The gold-embossed title had worn away here and there but was still legible.

'*The Treasure of Hollow Head.*'

The brass bell sounded, and an old man with a walking cane in one hand and a newspaper in the other tottered in.

'Good morning,' he said. 'I hope you haven't been waiting too long.'

'Not at all,' Kevin replied. 'We're just browsing.'

'Well, let me know if you need any help.'

'Cheers. Will do.'

'Should we ask him?' Neil whispered.

Kevin rubbed his chin for a moment before answering. 'I guess it can't hurt. Just play it cool and keep it general.'

Neil nodded.

They strolled over to the counter. The old man had started reading the newspaper. He looked up as they approached.

'We're interested in the history and legends of Hollow Head,' Kevin told him.

'Is that so?' the man replied. 'Are you looking for Captain Redmond's treasure?'

Kevin and Neil looked at each other.

The bookseller chuckled. 'No need to be coy about it. You're not the first treasure hunters to try.'

'You must think we're wasting our time,' Neil said.

'Not at all. I've always thought the treasure was out there, somewhere. You know the story, I suppose?'

'All we know is that there used to be a sea cave in Hollow Head and that the treasure is supposed to be hidden somewhere inside, but that there was a particularly wild storm in 1911 and a landslide blocked access to the cave.'

'That's right. Legend has it there's another entrance to the cave. Many people have sought it, but to no avail. Several treasure hunters have even dived around the head in search of a submerged opening, but nobody has found one, and a few of them have died trying. The fact of the matter is there doesn't seem to be any way of getting inside Hollow Head.'

'You think it's a lost cause then?'

'I'd say so. It's your decision though. Mind you, you'll want to be careful.'

'Why's that? Do you believe in the curse?'

The man shrugged. 'I see you've done your homework. No, I don't believe in curses. It's just that I've lived here all my life and I know the waters around these parts. They're capricious and unforgiving.

105

The ocean has claimed many lives at Hollow Head. You're aware there's wild weather on the way?'

Neil didn't reply. He glanced at the shelves behind the shopkeeper. When he looked back down, he could see sadness in the man's eyes.

'Do you want to buy that book?' he asked rather sharply.

Kevin hesitated. He had a feeling the map he'd pocketed would prove more useful than the book itself, but the old fellow was clearly a fountain of knowledge when it came to local history. If they bought the book, it would be easier to get more information out of him. It was a tactical decision.'

'Yes. I'd like to buy it.'

The receptionist at the Hollow Head Holiday Park didn't bother with small talk. She pushed the paperwork at Kevin and continued doing her crossword puzzle while he filled it out. Once he'd finished, she placed her plump hands on the counter and grunted as she pushed herself up. She grabbed a key from the rack behind her and gave it to Kevin without a word.

'Thank you,' Kevin said pointedly, rolling his eyes. The treasure hunters may not have been as squeaky clean as champagne flutes in a gourmet restaurant, but Kevin had made sure he taught Neil good manners.

Mary — her name according to the badge crookedly pinned to her blue blouse — just plopped herself back onto her chair and went back to her crossword.

Once inside their cabin, Neil grabbed two beers from the esky and unfolded the map on the kitchenette table. Its significance was immediately apparent. Hollow Head and the lighthouse were clearly marked, as was the site of the blocked entrance to the sea cave. Underneath the lighthouse, three words were scribbled.

'Supposed access point,' Kevin read aloud. 'Where?'

Neil took a swig of beer and then looked down through the neck of his bottle, as though the answer was somehow down there.

'What if,' he ventured, 'there's a tunnel leading straight down into the hollow.'

Kevin shook his head. 'What do you mean, from the lighthouse?'

'Yeah. I mean, the words are written under the lighthouse, as though referring to it.'

'It's not feasible though, is it?'

Neil shrugged and drank some more beer.

'We haven't read anything about that.'

'All the more reason to investigate the possibility. If nobody else knows about the tunnel, then they haven't tried to find it. We could be the first!'

'Don't forget the first of the three words,' Kevin reminded him, pointing at the map. '*Supposed.*'

'Yeah, but don't forget the bushranger bounty we found near Fang Rock after reading about a *supposed* underground creek. Our biggest find yet.'

'True.'

'And Captain Redmond's treasure is supposed to be much bigger.'

'You're right, son. We need to follow this up. The lighthouse is automated, isn't it?'

'Yes.'

'And the old bloke at the bookshop mentioned bad weather on the way, didn't he?'

'Yes, and he's spot on. We're due to have a massive storm tomorrow night.'

'Which rules out the likelihood of any technicians heading up there. Or any stargazers.'

'Or teenagers looking to get laid or stoned,' Neil added.

'That's it then. We'll pop up later tonight for a spot of recon and plan accordingly for tomorrow night.'

The holiday park was at the opposite end of the town from the lighthouse, but that suited them well. It was always best to keep one's target at a safe distance. At eight o'clock, after a light dinner, they walked along the beach. High above them at the far end, the beam of the lighthouse circled through the night sky. It was a warning to unseen ships out at sea, but for Kevin and Neil, it was a beacon drawing them closer.

To their left, foamy waves crashed against the beach. To their right, the esplanade was quiet. Only a few drunken voices reached them from the terrace of the Beachfront Hotel.

Once they had reached the end of the beach, they climbed over black boulders until they found a surfers' track leading up through the tangle of twisted trees. The walk up the headland was challenging, but once they reached the top, they were rewarded with a spectacular view of the ocean, the beach, and the township.

There was nobody else around. The only movement was that of the light above them.

Kevin nodded toward the red-painted wooden door, which was covered by a portico. They jogged over to it and found that it was padlocked.

'Do you reckon you can pick it, dad?'

'I can try. Keep watch for me.'

Kevin took a pair of latex gloves, a small torch, and a pouch from his backpack. He put the gloves on, switched the torch on, and selected a pick from the pouch.

No sooner had he shone the torch on the padlock than he turned to Neil in surprise.

'That's a bit sloppy.'

'What's that?'

'The padlock hasn't been clicked into place. It just *looks* like it's locked.'

He twisted the padlock and lifted it off before pushing the door open and stepping inside. Neil stayed outside to keep guard.

A staircase spiralled up into the lighthouse, but it was the other direction that Kevin was interested in. He needed to work out where, if anywhere, there could be a hidden entrance. There was a door to his right, presumably leading to a storage area. That seemed to be the best bet.

He tried the doorknob. It turned freely and the mechanism clicked.

Kevin pushed the door open and flashed his torch around the small room. He was about to step inside when a distinctive sound interrupted him. It was exactly like the hooting of an owl, but it wasn't, of course. It was the call produced by the whistle Neil used to communicate with his father at night. They had been using it for years, ever since Kevin bought it at an antique shop when Neil was just a toddler.

He dashed outside, keeping the torch pointed at the ground, and closed the door. He placed the padlock back on the door but didn't lock it.

'What is it, son?' he whispered.

'I think I can see headlights through the trees.'

Kevin looked down past the old keeper's house. A faint glow was fading in and out of view, brushing the tops of the distorted trees.

'Let's take cover,' Kevin said.

They darted into the trees and crouched.

Before long, the motor of an approaching van could be heard. It was groaning as it struggled up the steep road. The two men kept low as the vehicle slowed and rattled past them. It came to a halt between the lighthouse and the barrier that ran along the cliff edge. On the other side, there was a sheer drop of almost one hundred metres onto ragged volcanic rock and churning water. A young man and woman jumped out of the van and walked over to the barrier. The man climbed onto it, using a coin-operated telescope to help him up. He then pulled the woman up and put his arm around her.

'Well, that's put an end to tonight's foray,' Neil said.

'It has indeed. They'll be settling in for the night. Let's head back.'

They crept further into the trees and found the path leading back to the beach.

Back in their cabin, Neil asked his father what he'd seen in the lighthouse.

'I didn't have enough time to get a good look, but while we were walking, I thought about everything I noticed in the store room. It seems to be set up as a living quarters and looks as though it gets fairly regular use. There's a bed against the southern wall, a small desk on a carpet in the middle of the room, a large wooden chest against the western wall, a bench covered with charts against the northern wall, a full-length mirror and a painting of the lighthouse on the eastern wall. There's also a small drinks cabinet under the painting.

'That's impressive, dad. But it doesn't mean much, does it?'

'I guess not.'

'No indication of an entrance to an underground passage?'

Kevin smiled. 'I'm afraid not.'

'It isn't worth trying again tomorrow night, in that case. The map is probably a load of crap.'

Kevin shook his head. 'Don't give up so easily, Neil. I know a fellow who found a secret opening once, right in the middle of Launceston of all places. It was in a grand old manor. The entrance was hidden behind a longcase clock. It was a tight squeeze, but he managed to get through and into a secret room.'

'What did he find?'

'Nothing at all. The room was empty. At least, that was his story. The point is that hidden doorways and secret compartments aren't as rare as you might think. I'm not giving up on this map just yet.'

'Any ideas where the passage might be?'

'I have a theory or two. We can try them out tomorrow night. Let's sleep on it for now.'

They woke up early the following morning and strolled along the esplanade, looking for a decent café, but the only one they noticed was closed. They then ventured into the backstreets, hoping to discover a hidden gem, but after walking the length of several quiet streets, they gave up.

'Let's sit down a minute,' Kevin suggested, pointing to where a jacaranda in bloom stood in the churchyard.

110

The ground the jacaranda shaded was covered in purple, trumpet-shaped flowers, and a wooden bench stood by its trunk. Separating the churchyard from the street was a low white picket fence with a rusty iron gate. There was a noticeboard beside the gate and its changeable letters read, FOR SALE.

The men crossed the road and took shelter under the tree. They sat on the bench and drank some water from their aluminium flasks.

After quenching his thirst and wiping his brow, Kevin turned his attention to the church. It was small and white, and the paintwork was peeling off the wood in places. Its stained glass windows were grimy and there were cobwebs on the bell frame that stood near the entrance. All around the church, the grass was long and thick.

'I'd say the church has been on the market for a while,' Kevin mused.

'I guess some developer will buy it eventually and build holiday units here.'

'Probably. I wonder where the flock goes for its Sunday sermon.'

Neil shrugged. 'There must be another church nearby.'

Kevin stood and strolled over to the abandoned building. He walked up the steps and kneeled at the door so that he could try to peek through the letter slot. A moment later, he returned to the shade of the tree.

'You thinking of buying it?' Neil teased. 'Isn't treasure hunting satisfying your spiritual needs?'

'Just curious,' Kevin said. 'There's nothing left inside except for a whopping big cross. The joint's empty. No pews. No organ. Nothing at all.'

'No hidden treasure?' Neil joked.

'Hidden, maybe.'

Kevin turned his attention back to the lighthouse. It didn't seem so mysterious under the hot summer sun, but he knew it would be after dark.

'I could do with a dip,' Neil said.

'Let's get going then.'

They left the churchyard and headed back toward the beach. A police car passed them on the way. The driver's window was down and the officer had a bored expression on his long face. He gave the strangers a disinterested nod.

At the beach, they saw a few surfers riding the big waves caused by a low-pressure system out at sea. They took their shoes off and walked down to the water.

'It's going to be a big storm tonight,' Neil pointed out, smiling.

'I can't wait,' Kevin replied.

In the evening, they went to the Beachfront Hotel and sat on the terrace, facing the lighthouse. Flashes of lightning could be seen out at sea.

There were only five other patrons at the pub. Two weary surfers were sitting at the bar, laughing with the barman, who kept glancing out at the terrace. There was also a burly man with tattoos covering his arms leaning against the bar. He seemed to be listening to the others. Seated at a table close to the toilets was an elderly couple. The waitress was taking their order. Once she'd jotted it down, she went over to Kevin and Neil.

'Hi, gents. Having dinner tonight?' She was an attractive young woman with long black hair and olive skin. Her eyes were sky blue, in contrast with the stormy firmament.

'Yes, please,' Neil answered with a smile.

She leaned toward them as she placed menus on the table. The men couldn't resist admiring her cleavage.

Once she'd gone, they looked at each other. Neil had a wide grin on his face, but his father's expression was more serious. He was frowning and biting his bottom lip.

'Are you right, dad?'

'Did you see her pendant?'

Neil chuckled. 'That's not what I was looking at.'

'I know. She has a spectacular rack, for sure. But her pendant.'

'Some kind of mirror.'

'Exactly. That's strange, isn't it?'

'I don't know. It might have a deep meaning.'

'A *deep* meaning,' Kevin repeated. 'Just what I was thinking.'

'You think it's a sign? You haven't gone all superstitious on me, have you?'

'No, of course not. It's just that it reminded me of the mirror in the store room,' Kevin explained quietly.

'You think that's the entrance?'

'It may very well be. Mirrors represented doorways to other planes of existence in ancient times.'

'You're going all mystical and superstitious. Watch out, dad. We're going to need clear heads tonight.'

Kevin nodded.

When she came back, they found themselves looking at the pendant again. It caught the reflection of a flash of lightning on its surface.

'Ahem.'

They looked up to find her frowning at them.

'What can I get you?'

'Do you have calamari?' Neil asked.

She shot him a look of pure disgust. 'I'm afraid we don't serve calamari here. We have prawns and oysters though.'

'Prawns will do, won't they, Neil?'

'Sure,' he said. 'Prawns with mayo.'

'And then?'

'The snapper for me,' Neil said.

'Make that two,' Kevin added.

They watched her walk away, admiring the way her hips swayed like seaweed in a gentle current.

The storm was drawing closer by the minute, and the bolts of lightning were becoming brighter and more defined. They hurried to finish their dinner while the waitress cleared the terrace and closed the shutters.

'It's going to be a nasty one,' she mused. 'You're staying at the holiday park?'

113

'Yes. I hope we can make it back in time,' Kevin replied as he paid the bill.

'If you hurry along now, you should be fine.'

A brilliant flash of lightning ripped through the air just beyond the breakers and the accompanying crash of thunder sounded three seconds later.

'Let's make a dash for it,' Neil said.

'Take care!' she called as they left.

But they didn't run back to their cabin. Neil had parked the van in an alley behind the pub.

The wind picked up all of a sudden as they drove along the esplanade. To their left, the slender palms lining the beach lurched maniacally. Neil struggled to keep the van steady as mighty gusts of wind buffeted it.

A small truck was heading into town along the esplanade. The driver dipped his headlights as he sped past. Seconds later, a car came out of nowhere and overtook them before disappearing into the darkness again.

'Everybody's in a panic to take shelter,' Neil observed. 'One thing's for sure. There won't be any horny backpackers getting in our way up there tonight.'

The wind grew in intensity as they reached the headland. The twisted sheoaks thrashed about as the van crawled up the road to the lighthouse. At the top, the force of the gale was so great it felt as though they would be blown into the raging sea.

As predicted, the backpackers were no longer there. Neil and Kevin were alone.

Lightning flashed overhead, making a mockery of the lighthouse's beam for a split second. The accompanying crack of thunder rattled the van.

'Bloody hell! Pull up by the door. Close as you can get. No need to sneak around on a night like this,' Kevin said, pulling a pair of latex gloves on.

He had to use all his strength to get the van door open against the wind. Once he'd squeezed out, it slammed shut behind him.

114

Keeping his head down and covering his face with his hands, he staggered over to the door. He checked the padlock and was relieved to find it was as he'd left it the previous night.

He turned back to the van and realised it was all he could see out there. It looked as though the portico and the van were the only two objects in existence, held in place by invisible anchors in a dark and turbulent world.

Neil fought to leave the van. Lightning struck, dangerously close, as he stumbled over to where his father waited by the door.

For an instant, Kevin's heart froze. The flash had framed his son like a photograph. It reminded him of a snapshot of Neil as a toddler, small and vulnerable as he learned to walk.

'Let's get inside!' Neil gasped.

Kevin closed and bolted the door behind them before switching his torch on. He shone it toward the stairs spiralling up to the lantern room. Then he swung it around to the door that lead to the store room.

Neil switched his electric lamp on and followed his father inside.

They stood without uttering a word for a minute, while the wind made the lighthouse howl, and thunder resonated. They studied the room. It was just as Kevin had described.

'The mirror.'

'You think so?'

'It has to be,' Kevin said, stepping toward it. 'A doorway to another world.'

He touched the frame, pressing it here and there, feeling for a secreted latch or button. Neil watched him patiently, hoping it would work.

'Don't just stand there, Neil. I might be wrong. Ferret around.'

Neil inspected the room. He looked under the carpet in case there was a trapdoor concealed. No such luck. He opened the wooden chest and furrowed through the tangle of spare parts and rusted trinkets inside. Nothing. He moved on to the drinks cabinet and decided they could do with nip to calm their nerves.

'There's only one bottle here, but it's a full bottle of The Kraken.

115

Good rum. Want a drop, dad?'

'Absolutely,' Kevin replied without turning his attention away from the mirror frame.

Neil opened the cabinet and took the bottle of spiced rum. On its label was a giant octopus with probing tentacles. He took a swig and then handed it to Kevin.

'That hits the spot,' Neil said.

'I wish *I* could hit the spot,' Kevin mused.

'Have you tried sliding it?'

'Sliding it?'

'Yeah. Try just sliding the whole thing.'

'It can't slide, Neil. There's not enough room on either side.'

'No. Upwards. Try sliding it up.'

Kevin held the mirror by the frame and pushed upwards.

He heard a loud click.

'What was that?' Neil asked. 'I'm right!'

Kevin grinned and pushed again. The mirror glided up to expose a doorway.

'Good one, Neil!'

'This is incredible! So, it has to be true. Captain Redmond's treasure is real.'

Kevin flashed his torch into the opening. A rope ladder with metal rungs was attached to the wall. He followed the ladder down with his torch and found that there was a rock shelf several metres below, but he couldn't see where it led.

'You want the honours, Neil?'

Neil took another swig of rum before handing the bottle to his father. He stepped through the doorway and climbed onto the ladder.

'Watch out for the ghost of Captain Redmond down there,' Kevin joked.

Once he'd reached the bottom, Neil stepped out of view. His lamplight quickly faded away.

'What can you see?' Kevin called.

There was no reply.

'Neil?' His voice echoed down the narrow shaft. He took a swig of rum while he waited for his son's reply, but only the howling of the wind reached his ears.

It must have been after a minute or two that he noticed the lamplight growing stronger again.

He breathed a sigh of relief.

Neil reappeared. He had a mysterious grin on his rum-soaked lips.

'What's down there?' Kevin asked.

'Well, I'll put it this way. They weren't wrong when they called this place Hollow Head. There's a passage about four or five metres long that looks like it was chiselled out. That must have given the poor bastards a blister or two. After that, the passage opens into a kind of fissure that leads downward. It appears to have been levelled out and widened in parts. I couldn't see how far down it goes, but it smells of salt water in there, and something else too, a kind of oily smell.'

'We'd better take a look then, hadn't we?'

Kevin stepped through the opening and climbed down the ladder. An almighty crash of thunder sounded as he reached the bottom.

They followed the passage and continued down along the fissure. The distinct smell of salt water grew stronger as they descended.

They could no longer hear the storm that raged outside or feel even the slightest breeze, but there was a subtle noise, muffled and rhythmic.

'Stop a minute,' Kevin said.

Neil, just in front of him, came to a halt.

They listened.

The sound came from below, still some distance away. It was pulsing.

'Water,' Kevin ventured. 'It's water lapping against rocks.'

'Yes, of course. That explains why we can smell the ocean. But there's no draught, so it must be coming from underneath.'

They started walking again, the torchlight and lamplight bobbing in the darkness. To their left, the wall of the cave curved inwards just above their heads. To their right, a lip of rock separated them from nothingness. As they continued down, the lip became less prominent until the crevice was a natural ramp. The sound of lapping water grew ever clearer.

'I don't feel too good, dad,' Neil said.

'Funny you should say that, mate. I'm starting to feel weak myself, like all my energy has been drained out of me. I wonder if it's that oily smell. The air down here mightn't be any good.'

Neil groaned softly.

'Stop a minute, son.'

Neil did as his father said.

They remained where they were and tried to breathe normally.

'It's not getting any better, is it?'

'No, dad,' Neil confirmed.

It wasn't the first time they had been in a tight spot together. In a way, that's how it had always been, the two of them lost in the dark.

'I'm getting weaker and weaker. It's as though I'm carrying my legs instead of them carrying me. We need to head back up before it's too late.'

But it was already too late.

'Illumination!' a voice called. It echoed throughout the cave.

In perfect synchronisation, several flames were ignited.

'What the hell?' Kevin gasped.

Neil said nothing. He just stared, dazed and confused.

There were dozens of oil lamps hanging from short chains attached to the cave wall with steel brackets. Several more were dangling from T-shaped frames further to the right. Standing beside each oil lamp was a resident of Hollow Head, and each was looking at Neil and Kevin with a passive, silent face.

'Let's get out of here!' Kevin managed to say, but they turned to find the route back to the lighthouse blocked. The policeman, still looking as bored as he had that morning, was standing next to the tattooed man from the pub. They were looking at the treasure hunters, their faces expressionless. A fishing net was stretched out in front of them, ready to be cast.

'It's not the air,' the voice said. They turned around again but

118

couldn't see who was speaking. 'It's the rum. Don't you know you should never drink on the job? Of course, they all do. They always do.'

Neil and Kevin locked eyes and tried to focus. They knew that they should have been in a state of panic or a fit of pure rage, but the drug had numbed their survival instincts.

'Who are you?' Neil asked, but even that simple question required so much energy.

'Come down here and you'll find out. We'll tell you everything.'

Neil dropped his lamp, carrying it required too much effort. Kevin did the same, letting his torch fall to the ground.

A shove from behind got them moving. They stumbled down to the end of the ramp where the rock floor became flat and smooth.

The entire cave was visible now, and their stomachs tightened as understanding dawned. There was no hidden treasure, and probably never had been. It was all a spectacular trap.

Halfway across, the cave floor disappeared, replaced by lapping water. There was a podium, carved out of the rock surface, not far from where the very centre of the cave would be, and a wooden crane with a winch was fastened next to it. Church pews faced the podium just as they would have faced the pulpit in Hollow Head's previous place of worship, and the organ, which looked as though it had been taken apart and later clumsily reassembled, stood to one side. An elderly man sat at the organ, ready to play, and about a hundred silent residents occupied the pews.

'Welcome to our temple,' the voice said as one of the worshippers stood up from a pew near the podium and turned around.

Kevin recognised the voice before he saw the man's face.

'You're the bloke from the bookshop.'

The old man smiled. 'I'm glad to see you found the treasure map. By the way, do you have it on you?'

Kevin said nothing. Father and son were both trying to work out what was happening, but their minds were dull.

The bookseller nodded to the policeman, who rummaged through Kevin's pockets until he found the map.

119

'You'll put that back in the book?' Kevin asked. 'No. But you can't. I have the book.'

'I have the book. Mary found it in your cabin.'

'Mary?'

'She runs the campsite.'

Kevin nodded slowly.

'You're all involved,' Neil mumbled.

'We're not the first,' Kevin said.

'Far from it, my friend. The legend of Captain Redmond may or may not be true, but there has never been any trace of his treasure found here at Hollow Head. For nearly one hundred and thirty years, The Cult of the Kraken has been encouraging the belief to lure people like you down here to our place of worship.

'We saw you looking into the church this morning. For many decades, we continued the pretence of holding Sunday sermons, so as not to arouse suspicion. These days, of course, churches are up for sale all around the country.'

Kevin and Neil found themselves staring past the bookseller to the surface of the sea pool. They had heard legends of a sea creature called the kraken, but surely nobody in their right mind could actually believe in such superstitions.

'You worship the kraken? That's ridiculous. People don't believe in sea monsters in this day and age,' Kevin said.

'Ridiculous, is it? Well, my good man, there are vast numbers of humans who still spend hours every week praying in churches, mosques, synagogues, and temples to various sky fairies, some of which are supposed to have written holy books. Millions upon millions of human beings adamantly believe this, right now, *in this day and age*. What is more, their religions are based on primitive superstitions. Ours is based on empirical evidence, tried and tested.'

Kevin had to admit that he had a point.

'You may be wondering, why the kraken?'

'Yes,' they replied in unison, barely whispering.

'Soon after Hollow Head was founded in 1882, the townsfolk began to notice that the sea was claiming lives on a regular basis.

120

The regularity of the deaths was bewildering. Every three lunar months, shortly after the new moon, a resident disappeared, usually a fisherman. The founder of the cult was Hollow Head's schoolmaster, George Margate. He was an amateur astronomer and well-educated in all branches of science. He also had a keen interest in marine biology, and much to the disapproval of our church's last god-fearing minister, he was an avid follower of Charles Darwin. It was he who first conducted a thorough survey of this sea cave and beheld the almighty kraken that dwells within its waters.'

'Hail the kraken!' the worshippers chorused. Their unified voice resonated.

'One night, an out-of-towner who had indulged in too much rum broke into the home of a local widow and raped her. He was caught and beaten by fishermen who had worked with her late husband, and they would have killed him had George and one of the constables not heard all the commotion and arrived in time. The precise details of what followed are not clear, but we do know that George managed to take the fiend into his custody. To put it quite bluntly, he was led to the sea cave and sacrificed.'

Kevin sucked in a sharp breath.

Neil groaned.

'I think you know what happened, or rather didn't happen, as a result. Nobody was claimed by the sea after the new moon.'

The bookseller paused and indicated the congregation with the sweep of his hand.

'Since that day, every inhabitant of Hollow Head has been a member of The Cult of the Kraken. We ensure that none of us are taken by the almighty one by offering him regular sacrifices. Tonight, the honour is all yours.'

The men listened, too doped to react.

'Now and then, we failed to make a timely sacrifice. The last time we allowed that was the saddest day in living memory. We lost an angel. You noticed the photographs in the bookshop. You saw the beautiful young woman. She was my granddaughter, the only child of our town's policeman. That was fifteen years ago, but my son and

I still shed a tear for her every day.'

The bookseller glanced at the salt water lapping at the cave floor and wondered how many tears it would take to fill the ocean. Then he turned back to his captive audience.

'In the wake of that terrible mistake, the good folk of Hollow Head made a solemn oath to each other. Never again, we swore, would we lose another son or daughter to the almighty one. They must always be free to surf and swim without danger.'

Kevin looked at the faces of the townsfolk, hoping to find a hint of pity or guilt, but they remained impassive and he couldn't think clearly enough to even attempt an articulate appeal for clemency.

'Antea, we're ready,' the bookseller said.

The waitress from the Beachfront Hotel rose and walked over to the edge of the pool. She wore a long black dress, and her arms were adorned with silver bracelets that snaked from her wrists to her elbows. The water, flickering in the lamplight, licked at her bare feet. She held her arms out in front of her with her palms facing downward, and for a moment, remained like that, motionless. Then, with a graceful curlicue, she raised her hands up into the air and began to sing. Her voice was glorious and the words she sang were in another tongue.

'Bring them to the dais,' the bookseller commanded.

Kevin and Neil were taken by the arms and propelled forward. The policeman and the man from the pub dragged them up onto the rock and pulled their hands up above their heads. The men resisted, trying to squirm away, but it was futile. Their hands were strapped to a ring hanging from the crane.

The bookseller strode over to the crane and started working the winch as the two captors stepped down from the platform. With a loud groan that insulted the terrifying beauty of the song, the crane began to swing out over the water and the men found themselves dangling.

They could see the waitress from the front now. Her arms were constantly moving, but the bracelets she wore could be seen more clearly. They were silver tentacles. The plunging neckline of her dress revealed her heavenly cleavage, but there was no longer a mirror nestled between her breasts. Her intricate amulet represented a giant octopus with probing tentacles complete with suckers.

She wasn't looking at the men, wriggling like worms on a hook. Her gaze and voice were being directed into the unfathomable depths of the pool.

The groaning of the crane ceased and was replaced by the horrible sound of rope rubbing against wood.

Kevin and Neil were being lowered.

The worshippers then joined the waitress in her invocation, and the church organist began playing a majestic but most unholy harmony. The dark music filled the cave.

As the terrified men entered the throbbing water, they felt their ankles and calves becoming entangled in a mass of thick appendages. Beneath the surface, it seemed that countless tentacles were squirming in the water, tugging them down.

DECLAN'S FANTASY

Declan knew perfectly well that he wasn't the only man in the world with a sexual fantasy, but he had to assume his was more specific than most. Ever since he could remember, without quite understanding just why, he'd had a thing for Asian girls. He'd always imagined himself taking an exotic wife, complete with monolid eyes and silky black hair, to Springbrook National Park to perform a particular sex act. The rules were crystal clear; she had to be Asian, they had to be married, and it had to take place in the cave called Natural Bridge at night, while glow worms silently cheered them on. Putting aside, for decency's sake, some of the finer details of just what the encounter would entail, it was quite romantic as sexual fantasies went and was undoubtedly the only remotely sentimental urge Declan had ever felt. This would have only made his secret desire seem even more perverse to his mates had he ever made the mistake of sharing it with them.

Declan and Katsumi had met at Platinum Nightclub, one of an infestation of hangouts where cashed-up bogan males stalked the females of their kind. He'd noticed her from behind; small feet in dangerously thin stilettos, shapely long legs leading up to a tight and unmistakably oriental arse that was clad in tiny red shorts. Further up, long black hair had caressed slender shoulders that looked like upturned teacups.

The instant her friend had rushed off to find a quiet corner where she could answer a phone call, Declan had seized the opportunity to move in before any of the other vultures who were circling could swoop on her. He was confident that the Ed Hardy sunglasses he insisted on wearing even when indoors, the matching flame skull T-shirt, the thick gold chain around his neck, and the tanned biceps he sported would be a combination no girl could resist.

As it turned out, he was spot on. He was exactly what Katsumi had been waiting for.

Their subsequent courtship had consisted of him showering her with extravagant but tacky gifts, fending off other males by flexing his muscles whenever a potential rival came too close, and trying not to make too many racist remarks or show his complete ignorance of Japanese culture. The first two had come naturally enough, but the third had been somewhat of a challenge.

Of course, none of that really mattered anyway. Both of them knew what they wanted, and they were getting it.

Before long, with Katsumi's visa about to expire, Declan decided to pop the question. She wouldn't be the first Asian girl he'd asked to tie the knot, but he had a good feeling about this one. He knew that she desperately wanted to stay in Australia, just as much as he wanted to play out the scenario that was always on his mind. Getting married for the sake of fulfilling a sexual fantasy didn't seem absurd to him. It was no big deal. Just another paper to sign. There was no more commitment involved in marriage than there was in getting a new credit card or paying off the car sound system. Most importantly of all, he could still sleep with other girls behind his wife's back, or even right under her nose if she happened to be cool with it.

He took her to an Italian restaurant and proposed while they were waiting for their tiramisus. She said yes and giggled affectedly while the other diners applauded. They took a selfie, her posing with the ring, and posted it immediately on Facebook. When their tiramisus arrived, Declan ordered a bottle of champagne.

In the morning, they planned a flashy beach ceremony for their wedding.

Once married, Declan couldn't bear the thought of waiting any longer. The following Tuesday, while they were having dinner, he told her about the cave.

'There's a magical place I really want to take you. It's called Natural Bridge. It's so romantic to go there at night. It's a cave with a waterfall flowing into it through a hole. We could swim under the glow worms and drink a glass of champagne. It'd be a kind of practice honeymoon,' he said.

They were to have a proper one later, in Thailand or Bali or somewhere like that where his boss had unofficial business contacts who would show them a good time.

'Two honeymoon!' she replied enthusiastically. 'Sound good. When can we go?'

'Let's go this Saturday.'

And so they did.

The day started at Surfer's Paradise Beach. Declan swam for a while, but Katsumi wouldn't go out very far. She was scared stiff of sharks, a fact he'd found amusing at first; didn't the Japs eat sharks, or was it whales? Same diff, he figured. She just splashed around in the breakers, and every now and then, when she noticed the water was getting up to the top of her slender thighs, she would turn around and wade closer to the shore.

After a while, once she'd had enough, she ran gingerly back to where her Hello Kitty beach towel lay and sat on it. Wearing a broad-brimmed straw hat to keep the sun from further tanning her face, she waited for Declan to come back to the safety of the sand.

He didn't leave her waiting very long. He never did. Just in case some surfer tried to chat her up.

'There aren't any sharks, Kats!' he tried to convince her. But she just looked at him, pouted like a little girl, and said, 'How you know that? Maybe they hiding. Maybe they waiting.'

'For you?'

She nodded. 'Maybe. Anyway, I getting brown skin here. Time to go inside.'

He wanted to make her as happy as he could. Everything depended on that.

'Do you want me to buy you something cute?'

She smiled and held out her delicate hands so that he could pull

126

her up.

Katsumi absolutely loved cute things. Anything pink or fluffy tickled her fancy, especially toys and clothes that looked like animals. Koalas fascinated her with their fuzzy ears and black button noses, as did lorikeets and rosellas with their colourful plumage.

Declan was also a shopaholic and had similarly garish tastes. He was obsessed with bling, loud shirts, and studded baseball caps.

The couple had three things in common; shopping, nightclubbing, and popping pills. They were faithful adherents to the religion of über-consumerism. But that was about all they had in common. Katsumi only tolerated the beach for Declan's sake. She was so adept at hiding her dislike for that most sun-drenched and shark-infested of places, and he was so oblivious to the subtlety of her nature, that he actually thought she quite liked sitting there on her towel and admiring his muscular body as he swam in the waves. Likewise, he was starting to get tired of her. Marriage had turned out to be more of a constraint than he'd expected. He hadn't banged any other girls in the weeks since they had met, except for a brief encounter in the toilets at Vanity Nightclub that Saturday night when Katsumi had gone to bed early. But both he and the girl had been off their nuts, so that hardly counted.

'Let's go to Pacific Fair!' he suggested.

'Good idea,' Katsumi agreed. 'I need boot for forest tonight. What you need?'

Declan was pretty sure he had everything required stashed away in the back of the car, carefully placed so as not to block the sound from his subwoofer and amps. There were some expensive snacks, a bottle of champers, a few pills, and some toys to play around with.

He grinned to himself.

Katsumi narrowed her eyes suspiciously, but said nothing.

He had more practical items too; a torch, a picnic blanket, toilet paper, a few towels, and a camera.

'I got everything I need, Kats. But all I really need is your company. Didn't you know?'

She smiled at him and made a puppy dog face, but as he kissed her pathetically on the cheek and squeezed what little there was of her right buttock, the cute expression quickly disappeared and she rolled her eyes to herself.

They headed over to Pacific Fair, Declan driving as fast as he could and weaving through traffic even though they were in no hurry at all. They spent all afternoon there, roaming countless boutiques and department stores, eating an early dinner at the food court, and watching *Fast & Furious 8* at the cinema.

The whole time, every single moment that passed as afternoon dragged its heels towards evening, Declan was thinking about his fantasy. He was buttering Katsumi up like a Christmas turkey, and she knew it, naturally enough. She didn't know exactly what he had on his mind but could smell his eagerness. She guessed it had something to do with sex, and although that didn't particularly interest her, it was no bother either. She was just playing along, letting him buy her whatever she wanted and letting him think she was oblivious to his little game.

Daylight was fading when they emerged from the shopping centre with several bags of clothes and stuffed toys. Katsumi's intention of finding a pair of practical boots for walking in the rainforest after dark had gone wrong somewhere along the way and she'd ended up opting for a pair of bright pink imitation Uggs. That hadn't been part of Declan's fantasy, but he had to admit they looked mighty sexy on her, and, at any rate, it hardly mattered, because she wouldn't be wearing anything at all by the time they were under the waterfall at Natural Bridge. He could imagine the scene already, crystalline mountain water flowing through her black hair and down her back, gushing between her arse cheeks. The water would be cold, but she wouldn't notice, not with the special pills he was going to slip into her champagne.

As soon as they were in the car, Declan got the sound system pumping so that everybody in the car park could enjoy the compositions of David Guetta. Then he revved the motor so they could admire its powerful roar.

'David Guetta again?'

'You know the rules, Kats. When I'm driving, I choose.'

No sooner had he spoken than he remembered what he was supposed to be doing.

'But you always drive,' she complained.

'Hey, how about I let you put whatever you want on after this track?'

'Deal!' she chirped.

He silently congratulated himself.

'All right, let's hit the road, baby!'

And with that, he sped out of the car park, narrowly missing a woman and her young daughter on a pedestrian crossing.

By running a couple of red lights and overtaking cars in the oncoming traffic lane, Declan was able to make it to the Gooding Drive roundabout in record time. He knew for a fact there was no surer way of getting a girl in the mood for hanky-panky than proving one's manliness through motoring prowess. As he sent the car powering around the roundabout, Katsumi noticed the sun was on the point of vanishing behind the jagged horizon of the Scenic Rim. Darkness was already starting to sweep down across the eastern seaboard. They were about to enter a world of magic and mystery, and as much as she loved the glitter and bustle of the Gold Coast, she was looking forward to spending a few hours in this other place.

The road leading up into the mountains was winding and empty. Declan took full advantage of the conditions to zoom along like a V8 Supercar driver. They both had their windows down and Pink was squawking even louder than the cockatoos and rosellas settling on the branches overhead. Katsumi was singing along, approximating the lyrics without an ounce of self-consciousness. Declan wanted her to shut the fuck up but forced himself to hold his tongue. He was far too close to his goal to go and ruin everything now.

'So cute! Oh, so cute!' Katsumi started chanting. She turned the music down. 'What that? Declan, what is cute one?'

She was bouncing in her seat and moaning excitedly. Declan found it a massive turn-on when she got all excited like that. It made him jealous of the passenger seat.

He'd seen what it was as they whizzed past; a little animal by the roadside, between a low rock face and a reflective delineator post.

'That a baby wallaby?' she asked.

'No, it's called a pademelon,' he informed her, proud of himself for knowing.

'Another one!' she shouted.

'Yeah, there are lots of them up here,' he said, trying not to laugh at her. As far as Declan was concerned, they were about as exciting as Mother Teresa in a strip club.

'I love it,' she said, looking at him, wondering why he didn't share her enthusiasm. 'It so little and cute.'

'I know,' he replied flatly, and accelerated into a corner. The force pushed Katsumi back into her seat.

She didn't turn the music back up. She didn't say another word either. All she did was look through the windscreen at the trees and delineator posts as they flashed past, caught in the car's headlights for a fleeting moment. There were more pademelons, but she admired them in silence, lost in thoughts that were only coming to her now that she was away from the mind-numbing distractions of the coast.

Declan glanced at her for a moment, discomforted by her silence, worried by the fact that she was thinking more than usual. He reached down and turned the music back up, hoping that Katsumi would snap out of it and go back to imitating Pink.

She didn't.

Instead, a look of shock deformed her face, making circles of her eyes and mouth.

Declan switched his attention back to the road.

He knew the rule about animals. First of all, don't slam the breaks on, and above all, don't swerve. The idea was to just keep on rolling as though there was nothing there at all. This was especially true when the animal in question was a mere pademelon that would barely leave a scratch on the front bumper. On the other hand, he also knew that if he crushed it, Katsumi would be too distraught to

130

go through with the fantasy.

He had to make a quick decision.

He made the wrong one.

As the car veered towards the edge of the road, to where the ground gave way to trees and darkness, Katsumi gasped.

Declan was sure he'd swerved correctly and had enough time to brake.

He almost did.

But as the car came grinding to a halt between the trunks of two trees and it seemed that everything was going to be all right, the tyres lost traction. The vehicle went sliding to the right.

A low branch that had been snapped off, perhaps by a gust of wind, was sticking out from one of the trees, the one to the right. It was at just the right height and angle to poke through the open driver's side window.

The car kissed the trunk with no more than a whisper as smooth metal buckled delicately under the strength of ancient wood. It was a whisper that went unheard, smothered by the music roaring from the subwoofer and amps.

Despite the insignificance of the damage done to the front right-hand side of the car and the driver's door, Declan would have been devastated. Once, he'd almost lost his cool and punched a little boy when a football bounced onto his car's bonnet. He hated the thought of even the most insignificant dent disfiguring his cherished automobile.

And indeed, perhaps he'd been fleetingly devastated. Or maybe it was the knowledge that he would never have the chance to make his fantasy come true that had occupied his mind in that terrible instant. Or even a sense of profound regret as he realised he shouldn't have tried to avoid the pademelon.

The pointed branch had been lined up with diabolical precision and had pinned Declan to the back of his seat. There had been no cry of pain. Not even a groan. At least, not one loud enough to be heard over the music.

Once she'd breathed a sigh of relief, Katsumi looked to her right.

She'd been expecting Declan to be fine, but what she saw made her snap her eyes shut.

She saw the terrible image on the back of her eyelids.

There was no doubt about it, none whatsoever; her husband was dead.

She could feel herself starting to shake, so she took a deep breath and tried to calm down before she forced her eyes open again.

Yes, still dead.

She looked at the stereo console and reached down to silence Pink.

When she turned back to him, she assured herself that there had been no change in position, not even the slightest.

Dead.

The corners of her little mouth twitched nervously up and down, unable to decide whether to form a grimace or a smile. After a moment, trembling fingers clutched at her handbag and then fumbled to open the car door, banging its edge against the tree trunk. She squeezed out and staggered away from the vehicle, crushing leaves and twigs under her pink boots.

The motor was still running and the headlights were still on. From where Katsumi stood, everything appeared to be normal.

As she felt around in her handbag, trying to find her phone and wondering whether it would even work so far from the nearest town, the corners of her lips stopped twitching.

They had come to a decision, all by themselves.

She was smiling.

Meanwhile, the pademelon, as innocent as a new-born baby and blissfully unaware that it had, on that particular occasion, been as deadly as a shark, was hopping away on its cute little legs. It vanished into the darkness of the lush forest.

FORGOTTEN FALLS

Tobias Schenker guided the old rental van around a hairpin bend and swerved to avoid a fallen tree. He struggled to retain control as the steering wheel bucked and the rear wheels lost traction for a moment. Although not yet dusk, it was already dark under the dense canopy of subtropical rainforest. With every turn, Schenker hoped he would arrive at his destination.

The van rattled as he took yet another awkward bend. It turned out to be the last one. The van's headlights made contact with the cabin, illuminating a weathered wall and grimy window with an impertinence that risked waking the dead.

It was immediately apparent that the cabin was smaller than he'd expected, and that the clearing in which it was supposed to be standing had long since been swallowed by voracious creepers and saplings. Thick branches hung ominously overhead and serpentine vines swung from them, tickling the buckled corrugated iron roof.

Schenker struggled to perform a three-point turn in the confined space and backed his van up to the steps leading to the cabin's narrow verandah.

He switched the headlights and motor off and climbed out.

Darkness was descending and flying foxes, having risen from their diurnal slumber, filled the sky. Their broad black wings beat the air and their eerie chirping was supported by the endless drone of countless unseen crickets.

He took an electric torch, an oil lamp, and a box of waterproof matches, and flicked the torch on as he turned towards the cabin. He studied every inch of it, paying particular attention to the dirty windows that looked out at him from under the hooded brow of the verandah roof. Windows, Schenker knew, were more than mere panes of glass designed to allow light into a building. They served another purpose altogether in his line of work.

He walked over to the stairs and closed his eyes as he ascended them; one, two, three.

Nothing.

He shone the torch along the verandah and noticed the rapid movement of something small and dark. A cockroach or spider.

The verandah was empty except for an old rocking chair that had obviously been white once upon a time. He held the beam of the torch steadily aimed at it for ten full seconds before bringing it sweeping around to the cabin's simple wooden door. He'd expected it to be unlocked. In fact, there was no knob or lock mechanism at all.

Schenker lit his oil lamp. The warm flickering glow gave instant life to that dead place and chased the shadows into the corners of the verandah. With his foot, he pushed the door open. Then, holding the torch and lamp up, he stepped inside the cabin and was immediately surprised by what he found. Whereas the verandah was barren save for that one rocking chair, the cabin was a clutter of rusted tools, tattered books, yellowed newspapers, and items of an esoteric nature. There was a ouija board and a pair of dowsing rods nestled among a stack of papers and photographs. These objects confirmed that Schenker wasn't the first who had come all the way out here with the intention of finding answers. The unexplained case of Forgotten Falls was, after all, well-known in ghost hunting circles.

Schenker put the lamp by the fireplace and hurried back to the van. He wanted to get settled in, have a feed, and get to work as quickly as he could. There was no time to waste. He didn't know how long he would be able to hold out in such a remote location, and if he were forced to go all the way back to the nearest town for supplies, his presence would no longer be a secret.

Seeking out manifestations of the spirit world was an obsession for him. He'd always been a curious man, one of those individuals who yearned to feel the fabric of the universe and discover the sense, if indeed there was one, behind all the terrible absurdity of the world that was familiar to humankind. This respectable curiosity had been dragged down into the depths of obsession precisely three years, two months, and sixteen days ago. It was the result of one moment, an insignificant instant in the vastness of time and space, but one that had shattered Schenker's existence. His reaction had been to take time off work as a research fellow at the University of Munich, never to return. He'd felt the urgent need to be in isolation. After a month of mourning in the Black Forest, stewing green amanita and brewing water hemlock like a character from a Gothic fairy tale, he'd changed his mind and decided against *selbstmord*. He had so many questions that were screaming out for answers, and the terrible emptiness that his loss had left provided the freedom he needed to attempt to answer them.

Schenker set the gas stove by the fireplace, placed a pot on it, and poured some baked beans into it. Despite the summer heat, he wanted a warm meal.

While he waited, he rummaged through the photographs and maps next to the ouija board. He found a tattered map of the track leading to Forgotten Falls and was pleased to see it was much more detailed than the one he'd brought with him. The position of the cabin on top of one of the peaks to the southwest was clearly marked. He examined it carefully before folding it neatly and putting it to one side.

He then thumbed through the black and white photographs. Three of them showed a group of men searching around the waterfall, mist forming strange shapes over the rocks jutting up from the pool. They all carried long sticks and their faces were shadows under broad-brimmed straw hats.

Another photograph was of a mother carrying an infant girl, taken from a vantage point that could very well have been by the top of the waterfall. Both of them wore pretty floral dresses, and the mother wore a pair of horn-rimmed sunglasses. Schenker flipped the picture over and discovered the confirmation of what he suspected. Written in perfect cursive were the words; *Emily Fairley and daughter, Martha, 1956.*

He hurried over to the gas stove and turned the flame down a little before stirring the beans and adding an egg.

A sudden crash made the rusty roof rattle.

Schenker jumped out of his skin. Then, remembering the vines and branches hanging overhead, he relaxed. A thick tangle, a seed pod, or a rotten branch must have fallen. It probably wasn't anything to worry about; at worst, a python. He chased the thought out of his head. No, he reasoned, pythons slither and climb, they don't drop. He would have to get used to it. Stuck in the middle of a subtropical rainforest, he was bound to hear all kinds of noises during the night, interrupting the steady hum of the cricket chant. His presence had most certainly not gone unnoticed by the local wildlife.

'Und die Geister?' Schenker wondered aloud.

The crickets silenced themselves for a fleeting moment. Perhaps as a result of hearing a human voice for the first time, he supposed, if indeed they could hear him at all.

He glanced at the windows, but they reflected only the steady light of the oil lamp, and nothing else beyond or within the confines of the cabin.

Then, closing his eyes, he concentrated on the fine hairs on his forearms and the nape of his neck. But the air was still and the temperature remained constant.

He opened his eyes and frowned.

After turning the gas off and pouring the beans and egg into a tin plate, he took the oil lamp and went out to the verandah. Since his arrival, a gentle breeze had picked up. The uncountable leaves of the rainforest that stretched out all around him were rustling. Directly overhead, between the edge of the verandah and his van, Schenker could see clear sky sprinkled with bright stars that seemed to be almost within reaching distance. Of course, that was just trickery of perception. It was one of the many cosmic illusions that Schenker's inquiring mind so desperately sought to comprehend. Although he hadn't studied astronomy or physics in any formal capacity, he knew very well that the distance between the planets and stars could be calculated in light years, just as the distance between his former home in Starnberg and his present location on a remote mountain range in Queensland could be measured in kilometres or miles. That was all very well, but he yearned to fathom less tangible distances, such as the divide that separated parallel universes or planes, or the one that cut the living off from the dead.

Schenker walked over to the rocking chair and placed his oil lamp at a safe distance of about a metre beside it. The chair appeared to be moving, ever so slightly, in the breeze.

He sat down, closed his eyes, and pictured the Fairley mother and infant. Time too was a form of distance. Many years stretched between 1956 and 2016, and yet, a thousand people could have sat on that very rocking chair for all he knew. In some strange way, putting time aside, they could all be there together at once.

He opened his eyes again and began to eat his simple meal. There wasn't much more he could do that night. In the morning, he would start the long hike to Forgotten Falls.

Schenker didn't check the time, for it mattered not, but it must have been only a few minutes past eight when he crawled into his sleeping bag and closed his eyes. That night, he slept more soundly than usual and barely even twitched when a possum landed heavily on the roof and scurried down onto the verandah in search of a stray baked bean or two.

The mocking laughter of kookaburras roused him just before dawn, and in that muddled time between night and day, his eyes still closed and his mind confused as to whether it was still floating in the dream world or had climbed back into this one, he tried to reach out beside him, but couldn't. He was tangled up in his sleeping bag, and he was alone.

He opened his eyes and immediately wished he hadn't woken up at all, just as he did every morning. It was at that time of transition that the longing for what he'd lost and the absurdity of existence was keenest. He continued to be in the world, but was no longer a part of it. Day after day, he woke up a prisoner to his melancholy freedom.

Once he'd eaten breakfast and cast himself into his obsession, it would all be more bearable.

He grabbed a small carton of UHT milk and a muesli bar, and went out to the verandah to face the derision of the kookaburras. The cottage and van were veiled in the last gloom of night, but to the east, speckled daylight was beginning to tickle the treetops. The air was fresh and a gentle breeze brushed the verandah, but the German, although still unfamiliar with the Australian landscape and climate, had already worked out that the pleasant summer mornings were deceptive. Within an hour or two, the sun would be beating down on the cabin's iron roof in full force. That wouldn't be a problem for Schenker though, for he would be gone by then, descending through the cool shade of the rainforest, heading for Forgotten Falls.

Once he'd finished his breakfast, he packed the essentials for the hike. He would need his gas stove, his torch and lamp, two bananas, a tin of beef stew and a tin of baked beans, plenty of water, toilet paper, several pairs of clean socks, a spare pair of boots, insect repellent, his first aid kit, and his sleeping bag.

Then he placed the map and photographs he'd found in the cabin in a waterproof sleeve and wrapped his camera in a plastic bag. He put a compass, a pair of binoculars, and a black and white kerchief around his neck, and slipped his silver-framed sunglasses into a mesh pocket in his backpack. Finally, but most importantly of all, he made sure he didn't forget the broad-brimmed black hat with red feather that he'd received for his fifth wedding anniversary. This was no mere accessory. It was a sacred relic and lucky charm. Schenker made a point of taking it everywhere he went. Not even the wedding ring he still wore with devotion could more poignantly symbolise his undying love.

Hat in hand, ready to embark on a ghost hunt unlike any he'd ever attempted before, Schenker glanced around the room and checked that he hadn't forgotten anything he might regret having left behind. His gaze fell upon the ouija board and he couldn't shake off the feeling that he ought to take it with him. This tool, venerated by spiritualists but ridiculed and misunderstood by the masses, had never enabled Schenker to make contact. However, he knew two mediums who had opened the unseen veil between planes on numerous occasions using it, and he did not doubt their detailed accounts of the séances.

He walked over to the table and took the board. There was no more room in his backpack for it, but he was able to attach it using straps. If Emily Fairley and her baby were where they were supposed to be, he wanted to afford himself every possibility of connecting with them.

Schenker left the cabin and stepped out into the morning light. He put his hat on and blew a kiss into the air before unfolding the map. The path he had to take started several metres from the north-eastern corner of the verandah, but he could see nothing but thickets and matted vines blocking access to the forest. He hoped that the path would become clearer as he walked forwards, but there was no trace of it. The only indications that any humans had passed that way were one faint footprint memorialised in a patch of hard earth and the jagged ends of vines and branches that had obviously been hacked off.

Schenker shook his head at himself. He hadn't thought to bring a machete.

He knelt down and looked at the solitary footprint. It had been made by a right foot hiking boot and the size was the same as his. He couldn't tell how old it was but assumed it had been made when the ground was wet.

Turning his gaze to the bushes in front of him, he could only hope that the undergrowth wasn't so dense under the canopy of the forest. He got up and strolled around until he found a branch that looked solid enough to use to thrash through the vines and bushes. With one swing of the branch and one determined step, he started his journey into the unknown.

The air was moist and cool under the canopy, and although he had to constantly step over, duck under, and weave through vines and roots, there was little undergrowth to hamper his progress. The path, if indeed there was one, eluded Schenker, but his compass kept him heading towards the waterfall and the rise and fall of the land as indicated on the map enabled him to maintain a rough idea of his position.

The strange calls of birds the German had never heard before came intermittently from around and above him. Some of them sang sweet melodies and others produced long, single notes. There was one particular species which let out a long crescendo with a short, sharp inflection at the end, like the cracking of a delicate whip designed to deliver pleasure rather than pain. Occasionally, he caught sight of tiny finches as they fluttered from vine to vine, cautiously watching the bizarre and clumsy creature wandering through their world.

He hoped he wouldn't see snakes, and looked carefully at every vine and root before getting too close to it.

After three hours of slow and steady hiking, mostly descending, Schenker arrived at an area of large, flat rocks. On the far side, the rocks came to an abrupt halt and there was a drop of several metres into a lush gully. According to his map, he was more than halfway to the waterfall and had, more or less, followed the actual path. This was the ideal place to stop for a light lunch and a short rest.

With a sigh of relief, he took his backpack off and sat down in a shady spot. The day was growing hotter by the minute but a refreshing breeze reached Schenker from a gap in the canopy directly above the edge of the rocky outcrop. He took his hat off and used it to fan his face.

Once he'd eaten a banana and drunk his lunchtime ration of water, he lay back on his sleeping bag and closed his eyes. He listened to the birds for a quarter of an hour but didn't let himself fall asleep.

After his rest, Schenker referred to his map again and noted the suggested method for reaching the gully below the rocks. He followed the course indicated, a path zigzagging its way through boulders along the eastern side of the rocky outcrop. It was easy going because no vegetation blocked his way.

At the end of the descent, he found himself in a fertile and humid gully so densely wooded it was dark like a grotto. An elevated ledge that had once been the path curved around the lowest point. Following this ledge proved to be the most challenging part of the hike thus far. As he struggled through a jumble of fallen mossy trunks and voracious strangler figs, Schenker began to wonder whether he might have to turn back and make camp on the rocky outcrop looming overhead. But he pressed on for what felt like an hour and was rewarded for his determination when he rounded the gully and climbed a short, steep incline.

The cool breeze that had soothed him during his pause for lunch reached him again and he could see, between the trunks of the trees just in front of him, a wide valley and a magnificent mountain on the other side. Eagles were soaring, and a constant and reassuring sound, so very different from the other irregular and unreliable noises of the forest, told Schenker he wasn't far from his journey's end.

He raised his binoculars, hoping to catch a glimpse of the waterfall, but it was impossible from where he stood. He referred to the map again and found that the path down to the waterfall was straight but very steep. The last leg was going to be tough.

He drank some water, raised his hat for an instant to allow the breeze to caress his scalp, and then began the descent.

The sound of water tumbling down from a great height grew louder and more wonderful with every step, and Schenker almost cried when he first caught sight of the pure liquid sparkling in the sunlight.

At the base of the waterfall, he found a pool that slowed the water's progress before allowing it to pass through a narrow gap. From there, a stream gushed downhill towards the east.

He took his backpack off and undressed before jumping into the pool.

The crisp water sent a shiver of ecstasy through his tired body, and that split second was the most beautiful he'd lived in many years.

Somewhere deep inside, he wished he didn't have to resurface.

But he held his breath and let himself float back up.

He climbed out and wandered around the pool, exploring the cliff face of the waterfall. He wanted to find a sign of those who had been there before him, and to comprehend how a mother and her baby could have ventured to such an inaccessible place. Could the hike have been that much easier back when the path was still clear?

Schenker removed the photo of Emily Fairley and her baby from the plastic sleeve and looked at it. Then he turned his attention to the mountain looming to the north. He couldn't be absolutely sure, but it looked like he'd been right. The picture had probably been taken from the top of the waterfall. He dug around in the plastic sleeve and took out another photograph, one he'd brought with him from Germany. It too showed a mother and child. They were not at a waterfall, but the pose and expression were eerily similar. In both photographs, the unbreakable bond between mother and daughter was palpable.

Schenker drew a deep breath and tried to hold it in. When he had to exhale, only emptiness remained inside him.

He kissed the photograph and placed it back inside the plastic sleeve.

The sun dropped behind the mountain at around four o'clock and the waterfall was transformed in the evening gloom. Its beauty remained, but the darkness that fell upon it was of both the physical and spiritual world. All was silent except for its steady roar.

After dinner by the pool, with the moon making a turbulent mirror of its surface, Schenker dug deep into his backpack and removed a tiny silver flask of absinthe. He placed it in front of him, next to his oil lamp. He read through the papers he had. In particular, he read with great respect the account of the last sighting of Emily Fairley on the 3rd of February, 2013. It was this weird account, one that had made no sense to anybody else, which had enthralled Schenker.

Kevin Logan, a bushwalker from Toowoomba, and a man who had before that day shown no interest in the spirit world, had been sleeping at Forgotten Falls when a woman's voice had disturbed him from his slumber. She'd whispered to him in a language he couldn't understand, but that he reported as sounding like German. Emily

Fairley had been as Anglo-Saxon as they come, the daughter of immigrants from a Devonshire fishing town and married to an Australian of British ancestry. When he'd first read that account, the mention of German and the date, that loathsome date, had made Schenker gasp at his laptop screen. It made no sense in terms of physical distance and contradicted everything he thought he knew about the attachment of the spirit to the location of death.

He took the ouija board and placed it by the oil lamp, then he unclasped his flask of absinthe and drained it to the last drop. For a fleeting moment, as Schenker drank the last drop, time seemed to freeze. The breeze stopped caressing his body and even the roar of the waterfall ceased. But, as he lowered the flask, all was as it had been before and he had to assume that the strong drink had merely claimed his senses for an instant. Water was still tumbling from far above, glinting magnificently in the moonlight. The rainforest around him was hidden in a deep and tenacious darkness. Its canopy was too dense for the moon's powerful beams to penetrate, and the feeble orange glow of his lamp only brushed the trunks of the nearest trees and the uneven surfaces of the prehistoric granite rocks that had been flung through the air in aeons past.

Schenker lifted the ouija board and balanced it on his lap. He placed his left hand lightly on the board, near the letter N, and made certain that his wedding ring was touching the surface. He then placed the index finger of his right hand on the planchette and began moving it anticlockwise around the board. In that strange place, Schenker was cut off from the rest of the world, but he hoped he was in proximity to another plane of existence, and that he would succeed in making contact. He was wearing his hat and only lamplight touched his face. He was giving the board his undivided attention.

He brought the planchette to a halt but kept his finger touching it before extending an invitation in German.

There was no movement from the planchette.

He spoke again, but still received no response.

He changed to English.

'Spirit, are you here with me? I wish to learn from you. I invite you to connect with me.'

The planchette remained immobile.

'Emily Fairley, please join me. I know you are here.'

Nothing. He opened his mouth to speak again, not knowing what words would come out.

'Anke? Bist du hier, Anke?'

Schenker kept his knees perfectly still and made certain that he continued to touch the planchette only very softly. He measured his breathing and tried to control his emotions.

'Du fehlst mir.'

Nothing happened. The board and planchette remained inert while the energy of the physical world, the cool breeze and waterfall, flowed endlessly.

'Ohne dich kann ich nicht leben, Anke!' Schenker howled into the night air.

There was an evanescent movement within the lush rainforest, quick and purposeful like a swooping owl, but Schenker did not see it. He'd closed his eyes.

Only one sound could be heard over the waterfall. It was a voice. It had echoed off the rocks and trees that surrounded him. It was his own, full of anguish and absurdity.

He growled in frustration and cast the ouija board away, sending it spinning through the air and slipping silently into the turbulent water.

The moon, beautiful beyond human comprehension yet so cold and callous that night, looked down on Schenker, observing him dispassionately while its light played in the waterfall and danced in the pool, luring him in. He extinguished the oil lamp so that only the moon's stony white glow could be seen and walked over to the mossy edge. The ouija board had not resurfaced and was now either rushing downstream or trapped at the bottom of that small but spirited body of water. He knew that it would be so easy to join it down there. He suspected that a single step would suffice, and that a headfirst dive would definitely deliver him into the depths. He stood there for what could have been a minute or an hour while the spray of the waterfall caressed his face like fairy fingers.

However long it was, the moment passed. He sat down at the pool's edge and let his legs dangle in the water. Before long, he fell asleep.

The first flash of lightning Schenker saw was in his dreams, but no sooner had he opened his eyes than he witnessed another bolt rip through the sky far above the waterfall. The crash of thunder that accompanied it echoed all around him and shook his bones. The surprise that accompanied his rude awakening was twofold. He tried to understand when and how he'd fallen asleep, and how the weather could have changed so abruptly, but his pondering was cut short by the sound of crashing water growing increasingly loud. The moon was no longer visible but another flash of lightning afforded Schenker a glimpse of the grey and watery wall as it came over the mountain. Thunder rocked the valley, and then another flash, immediately followed by yet another clap of thunder, lit the scene. The storm was directly overhead.

He scrambled to his feet and looked around for his hat but couldn't find it anywhere.

In an instant, the waterfall doubled in volume and the pool surged up over its rocky, mossy edge.

Schenker forgot about his hat. He was sure it had still been on his head when he fell asleep, but it was now nowhere to be seen. He hurried over to his oil lamp and backpack, picked them up, and dashed into the forest. He struggled to light his lamp and eventually succeeded. Then, using its meagre light to guide him through the dark, damp forest, he sought higher land. Within minutes, and despite slipping and stumbling over trunks, vines, and rocks, Schenker was far enough into the forest to hear the agitated calls of hidden birds over the awe-inspiring growling of the waterfall and the bellowing of thunder.

He continued further into the forest in search of a grotto or hollow where he could take shelter until dawn. Through the lamplight, he thought he could see a suitable spot, but a strange sound made him stop in his tracks, straddling a strangler fig.

His eyes widened and his clammy skin shivered.

He heard it again and shuddered, making the lamplight quiver against the trunks and vines surrounding him.

It was a sound that had no place in the forest, so far from the nearest town. It was a heart-breaking sound.

A baby was crying.

'Halo!' he shouted into the wilderness.

The sharp cry reached his ears again.

He drew a deep breath and felt electricity rush through every inch of his being. His fingers straightened and the lamp fell. Without bothering to pick it up, he rushed off deeper into the forest, towards where he fancied the sound was coming from. He was no longer thinking at all. His senses led him. His need to find what he'd lost dragged him through the trees, and over rocks and vines.

Something white moved through the darkness ahead of him and a clap of thunder boomed overhead, but Schenker didn't even consider the possibility that what he'd seen might have been a sliver of lightning reflected by a tree or rock.

He heard the call again. Yes, a baby. Emily's baby girl. Or, through some incomprehensible whim of metaphysical design, his own daughter.

'Sabrina? Papa ist hier!'

He tripped on a root and hit his head so heavily that he was disorientated for several long seconds. Then, stumbling to his feet, he heard the baby cry yet again. Looking out into utter darkness, he was sure he saw a woman standing in front of him, waiting for him.

'Anke! Meine Anke und meine Sabrina!'

Schenker, in a frenzy of pure ecstasy, rushed further into the forest, never to return.

Nobody came to Forgotten Falls until almost a year later.

'It's spectacular, Leigh,' Rob gasped, wiping sweat from his brow.

'Will you bring my sister here?'

Leigh chuckled. 'I think so, one day, but not for our honeymoon.'

'Fair enough. Newlyweds need a comfortable bed, I suppose, and plenty of cocktails.'

Just then, something caught Leigh's eye, over by the edge of the rock pool.

Rob followed his gaze.

'A hat?'

'Yeah,' Leigh said. 'Somebody must have lost it here.'

'It might belong to the person who parked the van at the cabin,' Rob ventured.

'I reckon you're right, mate. We'd better report it. Mind you, it won't do much good. We both saw the vines growing over its wheels. That van's been there for a bloody long time.'

Rob knelt down to inspect the hat. It was battered and sullied, but the red feather was unblemished.

'Poor bugger,' Leigh said.

'Hey, can you hear that?' Rob asked, looking up from the relic. 'It must be that bird you were telling me about. What did you say it was called?'

'The catbird. It's a weird little bugger, isn't it?'

'Very weird. It really does sound just like a cat.'

'Or a baby,' Leigh suggested.

Rob stared uneasily into the rainforest.

ANIMAL

Terry joined his wife on the deck. She was sitting on a white rocking chair with red cushions, positioned between a rustic table upon which six candles stood in a row, their flames like statues in the still evening air, and the railing beyond which was a sheer drop of five metres. As he handed her the wine glass containing sparkling water, candlelight added to the liquid's lustre.

'Thanks,' Briony whispered, turning her gaze from the moonlit leaves and branches that reached towards the railing.

He kissed her on the cheek and placed a hand on her abdomen.

'Can you feel her kicking?'

He nodded and knelt, bringing his lips close. 'I love you, sweetie. Daddy loves you.'

Briony purred with pleasure.

'You're going to be an amazing father, Tez. I'm sure of it.'

'I hope so,' he answered, looking out into the trees as though expecting the darkness to either confirm or deny his wife's words.

He kissed her belly.

'You're not a very good husband though,' she continued, looking at the glass of red wine in his hand. 'You told me you'd stop drinking while I couldn't.' She was only half joking.

'I know. Do you want me to pour the wine down the sink?'

She pushed against the railings with her feet and set the chair rocking.

'No, I don't. What I want is dinner. Is it going to be long? Pregnant women get cranky when they're hungry.'

'It's almost ready,' he assured her. 'I've cooked up some gristle for Chester too.'

'Where *is* Chester?'

Terry nodded towards the far end of the deck. Their dog was

sitting up straight in the corner, staring down into the backyard. His brown and white coat was glowing in the moonlight.

'What's going on with him? I'm worried, Tez.'

'We might have a snake in the yard.'

Briony stretched her legs out and brought the rocking chair to a sudden stop. 'Are you serious? You're telling your pregnant wife that there are snakes in the yard!'

'I said there might be. Yeah, it's possible. We live in Bardon after all. The suburb is known for carpet snakes. It's only a matter of time before one slithers onto our property. There's no need to worry. Just keep making sure the doors and windows are closed at night.'

'Chester?' Briony called. He glanced at her quickly before turning his attention back to the dense tangle of trees, shrubs, and vines below.

'Dinner should distract him,' Terry suggested.

He went inside, leaving Briony to contemplate the moonlit leaves again, and came back a moment later with a handful of gristle that he placed in Chester's bowl.

The dog wasn't interested. He just kept looking into the yard.

'Put the bowl in front of him,' Briony said. 'He'll eat it when he gets hungry enough.'

Terry was about to squeeze the bowl between Chester and the railing when a rustling in the leaves broke the silence.

Chester launched himself forwards, stuck his muzzle through the dowelling, and started barking. In his agitation, he kicked the bowl under the lower railing and sent it plummeting to the ground.

'Now, you've done it, Chester!' Terry complained. 'What's wrong with you these days?'

Chester kept barking into the darkness.

'Be quiet, Chester!' Briony pleaded.

Terry looked over the side of the railing and saw the bowl on a patch of rocky ground. It was shining in the moonlight and the morsels of gristle were scattered next to it.

'That was your dinner, boy,' Terry complained. 'I cooked it up just for you.'

Chester looked up at Terry and locked eyes with his master.

'What's the matter?'

With a whimper, the dog lowered his nose to where the bowl had been and sniffed.

'It's down there now,' Terry explained, pointing into the yard.

'Open the side door, honey. He might go down there.'

'You really think so?'

'It's worth a try. He needs to overcome his fear. He never used to have a problem with the yard.'

Terry grabbed Chester's collar and pulled him across the deck, through the kitchen, and to the side door. The dog offered no resistance. But when Terry opened the door, Chester started cowering away from it.

'Don't be silly. There's nothing out there.'

Chester whined.

'Watch me, boy,' Terry said, stepping out into the night. He descended the five steps and looked down the steep hillside into the tangle.

The dog refused to budge.

'Go and find your dinner!' Terry snapped.

Chester was having no more of it. He hurried back to the deck and sat down next to Briony.

'I can't believe it,' Terry muttered. 'My dog is neurotic.'

He stumbled down the side of the house, making leaves crunch and twigs snap under his feet, and carefully stepped over vines and rocks as he made his way to where Chester's bowl had landed.

He was under the deck and could hear the white rocking chair grinding against the wood planks. The buzzing of insects was all around him too.

Then another noise reached his ears. It was metallic and shrill, and entirely out of place. It took Terry a moment to realise what it was.

'Can you hear that, Bri?' he called up to his wife.

She stopped rocking. 'It sounds like a bell.'

'Yes. What is that?'

Chester erupted again, his frantic barking making it hard for them to continue talking.

Terry could no longer hear the bell. He had no idea where it had come from. He looked down into the dense vegetation of his yard and then up through the trees to where neighbouring houses stood on higher ground. Apart from a speck of orange light from distant windows here and there, he could only see the white light of the moon.

He continued towards where Chester's dinner was scattered across the ground and had started to wonder whether he ought to get specialist help for his four legged friend when he saw something so inexplicable it made him stop dead in his tracks.

Chester wasn't neurotic after all.

There was no gristle anywhere to be seen, and the bowl was shining in the moonlight. As far as Terry could tell, it had been licked perfectly clean.

Terry brewed his coffee stronger than usual the following morning. His sleep had been restless. Every time a possum had scurried across the roof or deck, and whenever two branches had rubbed together, it had roused him. Briony, tossing and turning, and getting up to go to the toilet incessantly, had disturbed him too, and he was sure that after each trip to the bathroom, she'd stood at the glass door to the deck for a moment and worried about what was out there in the suburban jungle. He was going to have to put an end to all that, and as soon as possible.

He drank his coffee on the deck and peered down into the dense vegetation, hoping to catch sight of the stray dog, but there were only birds among the branches and vines. After a second cup, he rushed to get ready for work, and, before kissing Briony goodbye, asked her to look down into the yard every now and then during the day.

She did just that, but nothing stirred.

It wasn't until after nightfall that the strange happenings got underway again. Chester caught wind of it first and let rip with a tirade of distraught barking. From time to time, when he paused, Terry and Briony heard loud growling that made their skin crawl. It was a brutish sound that lasted for several minutes and only stopped when the bell cut through the air, just as it had the previous night. At the same time, to their right, a window was slammed violently shut.

'What's going on?' Briony asked sotto voce.

Terry could only shake his head in bewilderment.

'I'll try to come home from work early tomorrow and give the yard a thorough search before dusk.'

'Please do,' Briony urged. 'I don't like this at all.'

'Don't worry, sweetie. You'll be fine. Getting stressed about it won't do you or the baby any good.'

He gazed into the trees, and Briony could read the concern on his face.

'It can't hurt you up here. Just don't go down there.'

'I wasn't planning to,' she assured him.

'Good. So, let's forget about it for tonight. How about I run you a bath to take your mind off it?'

Briony squeezed his arm and smiled.

Terry got home from work shortly after five o'clock and greeted Briony with one kiss on the lips and one on the belly. After that, he drank a glass of mineral water and changed into old clothes before heading down to the backyard.

Chester watched him intently from the deck as he ducked and squeezed his way through the thick tangle, pulling cobwebs off his face as he advanced.

It had been a long time since Terry had ventured into the yard. It took him more than a minute to penetrate just six metres into the underbrush, and he soon realised that he was further away from the house than he'd ever been before.

He turned around and looked back at the deck. It was mostly hidden from view behind thick, crooked boughs and slithering vines. He could barely see the frozen form of Chester.

Terry quickly turned back to the dense vegetation around him, aware that he'd felt uneasy during those seconds peering up at the deck. He'd been exposed, but to what precisely, he wasn't sure. He studied the ground as best he could, kicking at the vines around his ankles. He had to find some indication of what had been, or still was, in the yard. There would surely be faeces or bones somewhere if it was a wild dog.

A broken clothes peg was exposed as the toe of Terry's boot displaced a rotting branch. There was also an old empty beer bottle by the base of a eucalypt. Presumably, previous tenants had been in the habit of drinking down in the yard, as strange as that seemed. Or perhaps, somebody had tossed the bottle from the deck during a wild party.

A sudden movement made Terry take a step back in fright. His left heel caught on a thick vine and he couldn't stop himself from losing his balance.

As he landed on his arse, a small dark form dashed noisily through a clump of decaying leaves and darted past him, heading up the steep slope towards one of the properties that loomed over Terry's.

Hearing all the commotion, Chester unleashed a volley of barks.

Terry's gaze followed the form and he let out a sigh of relief upon seeing that it was just a scrub turkey.

He got to his feet and brushed the seat of his trousers before turning back towards the house.

'Is that what's been bothering you, boy? A turkey?'

Chester stopped barking.

But Terry knew there was more to it than that. Turkeys could make some strange noises, but they didn't produce the bloodcurdling growl that had been heard the previous night. Nor could they sound a bell.

Terry continued studying the ground. There had to be something out of place. But as he pushed his way further down into the yard,

153

he discovered nothing unusual, apart from the twisted remains of a blue balloon and a split tennis ball. For the first time, he could see the chain wire fence of the property that adjoined his at the rear and a corner of patio belonging to the house that stood upon it.

Between Terry and the fence was a sharp dip in the land. At the deepest point, there was a bog no bigger than a bathtub. It hadn't rained in weeks, but Terry wasn't going to risk sliding down the slope and into what looked like mud. Instead, he turned to his right and pushed his way through thick vines, moving in the direction of Chris' backyard.

Chris was a dickhead of a neighbour. He raced around the streets in his ute and roared loudly while he watched rugby league on the television. Then he had the gall to complain whenever Terry and Briony made the slightest noise. Chris' dog, Bronco, was named after the local rugby league team, and he spent most of his time in the yard, apparently not sharing Chester's concern about whatever was hiding there.

Terry was just about to edge his way between the trunks of two palm trees which were separated by a mossy rock when something red caught his attention. It stood out from all the earthy shades of brown, grey, and green, and made Terry stop in his tracks, with his right foot on the rock and his left hand gripping the slender but strong trunk of a palm tree.

He looked down and saw the carcass of a large possum spread-eagled over a smooth rock. He'd finally found the sign he'd been looking for, some evidence that there was indeed a wild dog roaming his yard. He knelt, frowning as he looked at the carcass. Its abdomen was ripped down the middle and its four limbs stretched out towards the ground. Its guts were hanging down between its hind legs, clinging to its tail, and its lungs were still in place. Other than that, it was empty.

After nightfall, Terry carefully positioned himself in a corner of the deck where he was cloaked in darkness. He sat in the white rocking chair, keeping a torch at the ready in his lap and a bowl of raw minced beef at his feet. He'd dropped a handful of the meat over the side of the deck and was waiting to hear the tell-tale growls that would announce the dog's arrival.

Through the windows separating the deck from the living room, he could see his wife stretched out on the couch with Chester snuggled up beside her, his muzzle resting on her growing belly. Every now and then, the dog would glance nervously through the window, but Briony refused to do likewise. She was engrossed in a reality show in which obese contestants vied to win a huge cash prize by losing the most weight. The coloured light from the television screen made a kaleidoscope of the white walls and her cotton pyjamas. She was trying not to think about the wild dog in the yard, but Terry knew the situation had rattled her and that she was counting on him to deal with it.

He turned back to the garden. The waning moon illuminated patches of branch, vine, and foliage in places where the canopy above was relatively sparse. Leaves whispered in the breeze and he watched one that had been detached spin through the air before dropping out of sight. Further downhill, two boughs groaned as they rubbed together, and unseen clothes that a neighbour had forgotten to take off the line were flapping somewhere to his left.

As Terry contemplated this nocturnal composition, his eyelids grew heavier and heavier, and within a minute, he'd nodded off.

A ruckus slapped him back into wakefulness. A possum was emitting a bloodcurdling shriek and Bronco was barking savagely into the yard from behind the fence. Terry rocked the chair forward and switched his torch on as he jumped to his feet. Chester came rushing out onto the deck and growled into the darkness.

'What is it, boy? What's out there?' Terry asked as he manoeuvred his torch.

The shrieking stopped abruptly, as though the possum's vocal cords had been torn out.

'What the fuck's going on?' Chris growled across the boundary.

'Get inside, Bronco!'

Bronco halted his ferocious tirade and let out three sharp yaps, but his master wasn't interested.

'You heard me!'

Bronco hurried up the back stairs, still snarling.

Terry remained silent and motionless. He didn't think Chris could see him where he was standing.

'Fucking neighbours,' Chris complained to himself, before slamming the back door shut.

Terry remained where he was for several minutes, staring into the yard. The breeze had died down and the leaves were rustling less vigorously.

At first, he thought he was imagining it, but with each strike, his doubt diminished. It was the bell. Its chimes sliced through the night air, emanating from one of the houses hidden on higher ground to his left, from the same direction as the flapping clothes.

A branch snapped loudly, and, through a gap in the foliage, Terry caught a glimpse of a pale form darting uphill. The last chime of the bell faded and was replaced with a faint metallic groan that ended abruptly with a clang. It was the unmistakable sound of a closing gate.

Terry continued his watch night after night, with Chester, nervous but vigilant, at his heels. Each day was hotter than the previous and the evenings were starting to feel stormy.

Darkness drowned the world early on Friday evening. No sooner had the sun dropped behind Mount Coot-tha than the stifling stillness of the afternoon air yielded to a breeze which grew ever stronger as a swirling mass of charcoal cloud rolled in from the west, dragging thunder like a ball and chain.

The birds kicked up a fuss when the wind suddenly picked up, a distressed cockatoo leading the riot. The wind's invisible claws took a stranglehold of the jacarandas, throttling them and sending purple flowers pirouetting through the air before plummeting to the ground to form a carpet of subtropical snow. The downpour started slowly with heavy drops hitting the roof and steaming the air. The atmosphere quickly became charged with electricity and the distinctive smell of rain. Thunder boomed more loudly, making the deck shake, and flashes of lightning rent the turbulent sky.

Terry sat on the rocking chair with a glass of whisky. Chester was cowering inside the house.

He tried not to think about what hid in his tangled garden and assumed that no mischief would take place on such a stormy night, when every living creature had taken shelter in a house, kennel, hollow, nest, or burrow of some description. He closed his eyes and listened to the hammering rain, the drumming thunder, the whistling of the wind, and the groan of rubbing branches. He raised his glass to his nose, filled his nostrils with its malty aroma, and then took a sip.

When he opened his eyes again, he saw a beam of light hit the trees to his right. It wasn't a brilliant flash, not lightning. It was steady and comparatively feeble, even though the headlights of his neighbour's Hilux were unnecessarily bright for city use. The engine was powerful too, and rumbled like baby thunder.

Terry found a sense of unease rising inside him. He'd never liked Chris, and the feeling was clearly mutual, but he sought to keep out of his way, to avoid confrontation. Briony had first brought his attention to the fact that Chris was becoming increasingly intrusive. Terry had got that impression too, but he'd told himself he was imagining it, that he was becoming paranoid, or susceptible, or something, and that it was certainly due to the fact that he was going to be a father soon. People were always talking about the hormonal changes women go through when they're pregnant. Surely, men also go through a metamorphosis, even if they're unaware of it. But it wasn't just that. Briony was right about their neighbour.

Was she afraid of him?

Terry raised his glass for another sip and realised he was clenching it hard. If it had been a wine glass, it would have shattered in his hand.

Chris had no right to make a pregnant woman feel threatened. She was building a nest for her child; a comfortable and safe home.

Terry turned around and looked through the living room window to find his wife lighting a stick of incense.

He made a silent promise to her.

The next time that creep speaks to either of us with even a hint of hostility, I'll stand up to him.

A crash of thunder shook the deck.

Briony was chopping carrots when three loud knocks resonated through the house, making her jump, and almost costing her several fingers.

'Terry! Who's that?' she whispered urgently.

He stared at the front door and could see a blurry silhouette on the other side of the frosted glass pane. He turned to Briony and saw fear in her eyes. She reminded him of a startled rabbit.

'Terry?'

Her hands were shaking and it was with great attention that she lowered the knife to the kitchen bench. She was becoming a nervous wreck.

'Hello? I know you're in!'

Bang, bang, bang. The door shuddered violently with each thump.

The voice was angry, and the fist promised pain.

'Who is it?' Terry called.

'Your neighbour. We need to talk,' the voice boomed.

Terry's suspicions were confirmed. His blood was already boiling, and he felt his gaze drawn to where the knife lay on the bench. But he drew a deep breath through flared nostrils and tried to take the reins.

'I'll open the door once you've calmed down, Chris.'

He was impressed by how collected he sounded considering the fact he was on the brink of pissing himself.

Chris' face was up against the glass.

Terry looked at Briony. She hesitated, then shrugged.

It was his call.

'I've calmed down,' Chris said through the pane, almost convincingly.

Terry walked over to the door and put on a brave face as he opened it. His neighbour was hefty and stood a head taller than him. If push came to shove, he could swat Terry like a fly.

'What's going on? You've got my wife all worried,' he said immediately, wanting to get the first word in.

'It's Bronco,' he accused. 'I can't find him anywhere.'

Terry hadn't been expecting that.

'The storm last night was pretty bad. It might have scared him so much he jumped the fence and escaped.'

Chris scowled at the suggestion.

'Storms don't scare Bronco,' he hissed.

'I understand how upset you must be,' Terry offered, disappointed with himself for being so damned diplomatic with the brute. Was it fear, or an urge to prove that he was the better man? 'I'd be devastated if I lost my Chester.'

Chris glared down his nose at his neighbour.

'If I see or hear anything, I'll let you know.'

It was still there, in Chris' gaze; accusation.

'Your dog's been making some bloody strange noises at night, hasn't he? Probably needs some training. A dog needs to know who the master is, right?'

Terry had been wondering when that particular bone was going to be picked. The moron had it all wrong.

'You can't think Chester is to blame for Bronco running away. He's good with other dogs and he can't get into your yard. It's got nothing to do with him. All that commotion going on, it's not Chester. He's stayed inside for days, too scared to go into the yard. I don't know what it is down there.'

Chris nodded fitfully, his eyes always fixed on Terry.

'Right you are, mate. It's not your dog. Guess it must be a fucking werewolf. That explains it all, doesn't it?'

Terry just looked at him, pretending not to be afraid, but he knew he wasn't doing a good job of it.

'Watch that mutt of yours,' Chris warned, his voice venomous.

'What's that supposed to mean?' Terry asked calmly.

Chris took a step closer and snarled like a savage dog, his mouth small and round. His breath reeked of stale tobacco and too much red meat.

'It means that if I find out the little bugger has hurt Bronco, I'll string it up by its guts!'

Terry felt his knees start to tremble and could only hope his neighbour didn't notice. He was at a loss for words, and anyway, he was sure his mouth was incapable of pronouncing a comprehensible sound.

Chris laughed cruelly as he looked past Terry, trying to see inside the house.

'While I'm at it, I'll give you and your bitch the same treatment.'

He stared at Terry, daring him to react. Then, satisfied with the effect of his threat, he sniffed loudly and walked away.

Terry sat on the deck the following evening, trying to remain calm as dark clouds and darker thoughts accompanied nightfall. The disappointment in himself was worse than the fear and anger. He'd broken his silent promise to Briony and he was failing as a father already. Chris had made a death threat, right there at the front door, and Terry had just stood there and taken it like a coward. There was no knowing how much Briony had overheard, but she'd accepted his reassurance that their neighbour was just upset about his dog and that she had no cause for concern.

Terry gazed into the tangled yard, where shadows were growing thicker by the minute. He also looked over to his neighbour's yard every now and then, but there was still no sign of Bronco. He had to wonder whether the wild dog had indeed mauled him to death, even though such a feat seemed unlikely. There was, of course, only one way to find out. Going down there would require a certain degree of courage, and would, in turn, restore a little of his dignity.

Distant thunder sounded, reminding him to hurry up and act.

He stood up quickly, before he could change his mind, and marched inside. Chester, sensing his intention, whined in protest, begging his master not to go down there.

'What's going on?' Briony asked.

'I need to go into the yard. I can't stand not knowing any longer.'

She smiled faintly.

And so, after donning old clothes and a pair of boots, and taking a hammer just in case, he ventured into the tangle.

Every now and then, thunder bellowed, but it was still distant. Overhead, the growing evening breeze made boughs sway and leaves whisper; their meaning beyond human comprehension. Terry tried to follow the same route as last time, using the hammer to push vines and branches aside. A scrub turkey startled him as he crashed through a clump of lantana, but he didn't lose his balance this time. He pushed on, telling himself it didn't matter that he hadn't brought a torch, because he wouldn't be long, and that the movement to his left was just a vine swinging in the breeze, not a python.

When he reached the bog, he looked into it, and let out a gasp that was immediately smothered by the sighing breeze. His eyes darted everywhere, and he turned his head this way and that. It was a natural reaction that ceased once he reminded himself that Bronco's carcass had been there some time already.

What he heard next put him on guard again and caused him to raise his hammer up over his right shoulder, ready to be deployed. At the same time, it sent Chester, watching nervously from the deck, into a barking frenzy.

The groan of the rusty gate replayed in Terry's mind for several seconds, mesmerising like an industrial tape loop.

He stared up through thick foliage, trying to locate its source, and caught a fleeting glimpse of a woman as she turned and walked away. She had grey hair tied in a bun, and she stooped a little. He couldn't be sure, but she reminded him of Margaret Garran, a local widow of considerable fame whose husband had committed suicide after filing for bankruptcy.

He kept a tight grip on his hammer as the beast approached. He could hear it growling louder and louder. Any second now, it would come into view, emerging into the enveloping night.

When it did, all Terry could do was stare wide-eyed.

It wasn't a dog at all. It was a young man. He had a tangle of brown hair wreaking chaos over a prominent brow and calculating eyes that hinted at spasmodic intelligence. He was stark naked, his pale skin glowing blue under an increasingly electric sky. His mouth was moving, but Terry couldn't tell whether he wanted to speak or was merely salivating. It was the mouth that held Terry's attention. He didn't want to examine the rest of the man's body.

'Who are you?' Terry whispered.

His head shook, but Terry didn't know whether it meant he didn't understand or wasn't interested in conversation.

'What the fuck is going on?' Chris asked.

Terry turned around to find his neighbour leaning against the fence.

'What's your problem?' Terry asked.

'Don't you fucking talk to me like that!' he growled. 'I'll cut you up good and proper.'

'You can't see him, can you?'

'Who?'

Terry grinned. There was a tree blocking his neighbour's view. He turned back to the manimal, who was now licking his lips and sniffing the night air.

A flash of lightning tore through the sky and reflected off something on his body. He wasn't completely naked after all, for there were metal contraptions on his hands. As far as Terry could tell, they were cruel gloves that replicated the claws of a carnivorous beast.

'Tasty,' Terry whispered, nodding enthusiastically.

'What are you saying? Speak up!' Chris insisted. 'Is Bronco there? I fucking knew it! Your mongrel mauled him.'

162

'Bronco's dead, Chris,' Terry informed him. 'That's how it is in the animal world.'

Chris was about to lose his mind. 'Is that how it is? I'll show you what an animal is! You and your bitch and your unborn runt are all dead meat, fucker!'

The manimal's sinewy muscles were flexing and he was drooling profusely. He looked at Terry, head cocked and eyes questioning.

'Tasty,' Terry said again, more loudly this time, more urgently. He made a show of licking his lips.

The manimal's eyes narrowed. He raised his metal claws. His appetite had been piqued.

LIKE SISTERS

'Keryn, we've been best friends for nearly twenty years now, haven't we?'

We were sitting at Smoked Paprika, our favourite breakfast spot. There wasn't much of a view because the café faced south, opening onto the constantly busy McGregor Terrace instead of offering a view over the lower-lying suburbs to the north. That didn't matter though. We went there for the great food, and the fact that there was never a crowd.

'I guess so,' she replied, looking up from the breakfast menu. 'We were in the sixth grade if I'm not mistaken. You were new to school. You'd just moved up from Grafton. You know what my first impression was?'

I shook my head even though I knew, even though I knew that she knew I knew. I wanted to encourage her to reminisce.

'I had a feeling we were destined to be together, that my dad had been transferred to Brisbane just so we would meet.'

'Like sisters separated at birth,' I added.

She smiled. That was how everybody described us, and it was true. But, at the same time, we were so very different. I was the stable one, the rock, whereas Keryn was always losing her way. Ever since high school, one hopeless boyfriend after another had sucked her in. Steve was the latest. He'd entered her life four months ago at a party neither of us should have gone to, and two months ago, they had suddenly decided to move in together.

'You've always been there for me despite the shit I keep getting myself into.'

'And you for me.'

She frowned. 'Yeah, but we both know it's mostly you doing the rescuing.'

I started fidgeting with the salt shaker, then, decisively, put it back down and spoke my mind.

'Keryn, the thing is, well, it's really worrying me this time. You've changed. He has changed you.'

She sighed and turned her attention back to the menu, hiding her face from me. But it didn't work. I noticed the grimace. It lasted just a fleeting moment. Her pencil-thin eyebrows rose and the now cracked corners of her mouth sank in as though she'd tasted something sour. I knew her every expression. I had to keep talking.

'Maybe you can't see it because you're inside it, Keryn. It's like when you go to an art gallery. To fully appreciate an epic tableau, you have to step back, right back. That's the only way to make sense of the big picture.'

Her face was blank. She wasn't impressed. Perhaps the metaphor was lost on her. After all, we hadn't been to a gallery together in years, and that was part of the problem. Too many Mr Wrongs had led her astray and crushed two of her most endearing characteristics; creativity and curiosity.

'I'm still me, honey. I haven't gone anywhere.'

Her eyes said otherwise.

'I'm a vet's assistant, remember? I'm trained to know when an animal is in distress. You've lost weight since you moved in with him and your hands tremble now.'

She looked at her hands, clasping the menu too tightly, and tried to keep them perfectly still. It was impossible. She clenched them into fists.

'What are you guys using? Heavy stuff?'

She bit her lip. She knew I hated drugs. Sure, we'd experimented at high school, just like everybody else, but I'd never made a habit of it. She had, but never to this extent.

'What are you doing with him?'

'I love him,' she told me, her eyes full of hopelessness.

I almost cringed. How could she possibly love Steve? He couldn't hold a job down and he hated that she could. He felt inferior to her and was using drugs as a means of making her dependent on him. It was obvious. It was the only thing he could offer her. And with drugs came violence more often than not. I couldn't help but wonder whether he was hitting her. There were bruises on her skinny forearms, and I found myself imagining that cruel, digging fingers had caused them.

'I love him,' she repeated. 'I know you don't approve, but I'm madly in love with him.'

Mad was the word.

Keryn lost her job two weeks later. She told me it was the result of cutbacks in the sales department, but I knew better. Her deterioration was accelerating. Her diet of drink and drugs was taking its toll. She would soon be nothing but skin, bones, and sallow eyes. We stopped going out for breakfast. We met at my house, and nowhere else.

One Saturday afternoon, we were sitting on my balcony, drinking coffee and watching passers-by on Given Terrace, when she dropped a bombshell.

'I have to tell you something,' she began.

'Yes?' I encouraged her warily.

'I've decided to have a baby.'

'What!'

'I'm not getting any younger. It's time.'

'Neither of us is getting any younger, but now is definitely *not* the time. You don't really want to start a family with Steve. I know you don't. Where's the Keryn I used to know?'

I stared into her eyes. They were pleading me. She needed me to save her from herself.

'I'm still here, but I want to have a child now.'

'With Steve? Tell me you want to start a family with him. Tell me!' I almost shouted at her.

'I want to have a child,' she hissed.

I noticed she was trembling.

166

'If you have a child with him, you'll be attached to him for the rest of your life. Whatever happens, it will be impossible to make a clean break.'

She said nothing, just looked down at the street.

'I have to do this.'

'Do you truly love him, Keryn? Just tell me that. Are you in love with this man?'

'You've already asked me that,' she answered.

'Please, tell me again,' I urged.

'I love him,' she said quietly, and again, her eyes told another story.

She was trapped. Love is addictive, just like any other drug. Love tells you how to feel and behave. You don't choose it. You stumble across it and it ensnares you, like quicksand.

'He's destroying you, sister. You're wasting away and you can't even see it. Please, just believe me.'

'Are you jealous? Is that what this is?' she asked me, and I immediately recognised it as a desperate ploy. We looked into each other's eyes. Mine told her that nothing could be further from the truth. Being alone was better than being enslaved and degraded. Hers told me that she felt helpless and lost.

'That was stupid,' she said. 'Can we just leave it for today?'

I didn't reply. Leave it for today. One day. But the problem would still be there tomorrow. In fact, it would be much worse then. She was withering away a little more every day. She thought she was making the decisions, but she wasn't.

I couldn't hold back any longer. I broke down and cried, leaning against the balcony railing. My tears would fall to the pavement, soaking it with sadness.

Keryn hugged me in her bruised, skeletal arms.

Steve threw a party the following Saturday night, just as he did every weekend. Before he'd come along and changed everything, we'd been in the habit of going out for dinner, two or three drinks, and to see a film or go to a gig. Not every Saturday, but most. In the past four months, we'd only been out twice; once to watch a suspense movie called *Nightcrawler*, and the other time to catch Infinite Void rocking at The Bearded Lady. Looking back now, I guess I should have figured out that those two names were trying to tell me something about what was happening to us; a creep had come to exploit my sister and leave me in a vacuum. He was like the villain from a fairy tale, except that he didn't have the obligatory sense of purpose, other than to hold Keryn spellbound. We'd never had the same taste in men, and I knew the type she went for, but I couldn't for the life of me identify one single redeeming feature in Steve. She found him sexy. She'd told me as much. But he was repugnant to me.

Even though I was tired from a particularly busy day, I decided to go to Steve's party for once. Keryn had asked me to come and would have started begging had I refused. I didn't want to lower her to that. She was low enough as it was. Anyway, we had a visceral need to be together that weekend more than ever. On top of that, the fact that Steve didn't want me there only reinforced my determination. We were fighting for Keryn's soul and one of us was bound to win eventually. Of course, he had the upper hand. His only skills, those of emotional manipulation and psychological corrosion, were so finely honed that even a friendship of twenty years couldn't withstand them.

I bought some chicken, green curry paste, and coconut milk on the way home from work. I knew there wouldn't be any decent food at Steve's place, and even if there was, I didn't want to accept anything from him. I sat on my balcony and enjoyed my dinner with a glass of crisp white wine while the traffic below headed east towards the bars of Caxton Street.

After dinner and a shower, I drove to the party and parked around the corner where I thought my car would be safe from the vandals who never missed their profane pilgrimage to Steve's. The area was quite nice. Most of the homes had mown lawns behind neat picket fences or flawlessly trimmed hedges. But his house stood out like an overlooked weed in an otherwise orderly rose garden. The fence was crooked and unpainted, and the lopsided letterbox vomited junk mail. Grass and thistles that were waist-high in places covered the front yard, and a corroded car body crouched under a frangipani tree in one corner. There was no path leading from the unhinged wrought-iron gate to the front stairs, only a narrow, trodden track.

I looked up at the moon, glorious in its pure radiance, before entering the property and cautiously following the track. I climbed the stairs and raised my finger to the doorbell only to find myself hesitant to make contact. A cacophony of thrash metal, shouting, and groaning assaulted me through the closed door. Every nerve in my body was urging me to hurry back to my car and drive home. I had to remind myself why I was there. For Keryn. She needed me there that night. She needed me more than ever.

My finger pressed the button and I heard the doorbell ring, defying the wall of noise.

It was the devil himself who answered. He looked me up and down, equal parts of lust and loathing evident in his gaze. He held a bottle of Jim Beam and cola in one hand and he was twitching it. I couldn't help but feel that he wanted to smash it over my head. Instead, he stepped back and let me in without so much as a word. He just looked down his powdered nose at me as I edged past and sniffed loudly like a dog picking up a scent.

Many of the thirty-odd guests were already drunk or passed out. Others were sitting on putrid couches or on the floor, rocking back and forth like lunatics.

I checked the time. It was just after eight o'clock.

I knew a handful of the women but didn't want to talk to any of them. The feeling would have been mutual, but they were too wasted to even notice me. A few of the men looked at me, violating me with their eyes. One seemed to make a move towards me, but stumbled over a woman sitting on the floor. She said nothing. She was in another world. I hurried off, eager to save us both from an awkward encounter.

It didn't take me long to find Keryn. She was in a corner of the back deck. There were other people around her, but she was alone, staring at the almost full moon. That seemed to make sense.

'How are you going, babe?'

She turned to me and smiled wearily. In just one week, she'd waned. 'Good, honey. How about you?'

'Better now that I've found you.'

'Did you see Steve?'

'Yes,' I replied. 'He let me in.'

'Did you talk to him?'

'We said hello to each other,' I lied.

She winked at me and turned her gaze back to the moon. I got the feeling she wanted to be up there. It wasn't such a bad idea.

'You never used to like this kind of music.'

'No. I still don't, but Steve does, and all his friends do too.'

'Can we go for a walk?'

She kept looking at the moon but reached out with her right hand and took hold of mine. Her bony fingers squeezed my hand desperately, as though she were hanging off the edge of a cliff.

'Just give me a few minutes. I need to go to the toilet,' I told her.

'I'll be right here.'

I had to push my way past people to get to the toilets and even step over somebody. I edged past Steve too. He was sitting on a couch with his back to me and his head bowed. The two guys beside him had their eyes closed. Under different circumstances, one could have been forgiven for thinking they were praying. But religion was certainly not their opiate of choice.

I paused for a moment, taking advantage of their wretched state, then kept on going until I got to the toilet, only to find the door locked.

I waited.

After a few minutes, I knocked on the door.

Somebody grunted.

I waited another minute and knocked again.

'Occu-fucking-pied!'

That was followed by a loud snort. Coke, I guessed.

I forgot about it and hurried back to Keryn. I didn't really need to piss anyway. What I needed was to get out of there, and take my sis with me.

There was a park just down the street. I generally avoided parks at night, but it seemed like a safe haven compared to Steve's place. Keryn was happy to go for a walk with me. We sat on a bench, hand in hand, and listened to leaves rustling in the breeze. A nearby owl was hooting and crickets were singing.

'I love it how we can have a conversation without even speaking,' she said.

'Me too.'

That's all we said. Keryn rested her head on my shoulder and we listened to nature's nocturnal symphony for minutes, hours, aeons. Time didn't matter. When our bums got sore, we lay on the grass.

Before long, we fell asleep.

It was Keryn's mobile that woke us.

'Steve,' she told me before answering.

'Hey, Steve, look, don't worry…'

She cut herself off and her moonlit face twisted.

'Who's this again?' she asked.

She listened.

'The hospital! I'm coming now… Why? What do you mean it's too late?'

I caught her in my arms.

When Keryn came to, I told her I would drive her to the hospital, but she decided not to go. Instead, she came home with me.

Neither of us slept much that night. Nor did we speak. The shock was too great.

In the morning, I made strong coffee and we drank it on my balcony.

'I don't know what to say, Ker.'

'I told you so, perhaps.'

171

'What kind of friend would say that?' I asked.

She sipped at her coffee. She was deep in thought. She hadn't cried and I knew that bothered her.

'I know we were only together for four months, but I should be devastated, right?'

'I can't pretend to know how you should feel. I've never loved a man the way you loved him.'

'That's the thing though. I didn't love him, did I? You tell me. I'm hardly devastated, am I? Maybe I'm just in shock, but I feel relieved.'

I could have told her that I wasn't surprised, but I resisted the temptation to say anything of the sort. Instead, I pursued her with, 'You told me you were madly in love with him. You said you wanted to have his baby.'

'I did. I said that. It was like I was another person.'

'You were under his spell.'

She nodded, staring into her mug. 'But now the spell is broken. The warlock overdosed on his own magic potion.'

I drank my coffee.

Keryn turned to me. She stared into my eyes.

'How has work been recently?' she asked.

I ought to have been taken aback by the sudden change in conversation, but I wasn't. Four months of Steve, of excessive drink and drugs, hadn't entirely numbed her mind.

'I've been busy, but it's been fine. I'm learning a lot.'

'You tell me about Francis, and about some of the pets and their owners, but I don't know much about what you really do.'

'You know what I do, Ker. I help animals get better. That's why I love my job so much. I can't describe the feeling I get when I save someone's pet.'

'Sometimes, I suppose, you can't help them.'

I nodded.

'Has that happened recently?'

'It has.'

'Have you put any dogs down recently?'

We held each other's gaze.

'Yes,' I said. 'One.'
She smiled faintly.
'Sometimes, it's the only solution,' I explained.
Her mouth formed no words, but her eyes thanked me.

IT STARTS WITH INSECTS

The boy pried at the big black beetle, trying to loosen its grip. But it wasn't going to let itself be taken without a fight. It had clawed limbs that anchored it to the tree's rough bark. The unfortunate insect had been randomly selected to participate in the boy's latest study, and the course of its simple and inconspicuous existence was about to be irreversibly altered. Its chances of surviving until nightfall were extremely slim.

He didn't pull too forcefully, because the subject would be of no use to him if he maimed or killed it before its time. It had to be fully functional. The pressure he applied was firm but reasonable.

Not far away – indeed much too close for his liking – dozens of children occupied themselves with more mundane activities. Some were swinging like primates from the climbing frame or playing football on the miniature pitch, laughing and shouting with the excitement generated by being released from the classroom. A negligent warden had left the asylum gates open, and the sudden release from captivity had exacerbated the patients' mental instability.

The park was only a block away from his school, so most of the other youngsters there were fellow classmates. But these lunatics were not his friends. He rarely spoke to them inside the classroom or in the playground, and never beyond the confines of school property. Several mothers were also in the park, surveying their children while they chatted and gossiped about other parents. Sometimes their words would reach the boy's ears, and he couldn't help but feel sorry for them with their petty intellects.

The beetle really was very determined. It just kept clinging, even though there was nothing it could do against the giant hand harassing it. The boy thought for a moment that its six appendages would end up being torn from its shell if it didn't let go, but he'd decided it was taking part in his study and he certainly wasn't going to be discouraged.

He was the one in control.

He eventually succeeded in forcing the beetle to loosen its grip without dismembering any of its limbs. It struggled ridiculously, scratching at thin air, but he dropped it into a glass jar he'd prepared that morning before going to school. He always organised his experiments in advance and ensured that everything he needed was in his schoolbag. That way, he wouldn't have to go home before coming to the park. In fact, he avoided going home as much as possible. His mum was always there with her new boyfriend, and more often than not he was either menacing her into submission or beating her black and blue. The other things, apart from the beatings, were unknown and unimaginable at his tender age.

'Good shot, Paul! I'll take the corner.'

He looked at the ball, which had rolled uncomfortably close, and sneered at the other boys, safe in the knowledge that they couldn't see him from the pitch. He didn't like them being anywhere near him when he was engaged in his studies. At best, they were blundering fools, but more often than not, they were wilfully destructive.

The beetle stumbled around in the glass jar, and the boy lifted it to eye level. He studied the way it was reacting to its new environment. One of the aims of the project was to identify how basic life forms coped with unusual circumstances and to measure their capacity to adapt to such changes.

'Good save!' one of the fathers commented from the sideline.

The boy glanced briefly towards the pitch before turning his attention back to his beetle, which was still moving clumsily around the circumference of the jar.

He'd never really known his father. He had some vague memories of him, but they were all bad ones. His mum told him his dad was scum and always would be, and that he was better off not bothering to think about him at all. But sometimes he couldn't help himself, especially when other kids' dads came to the park and played with them while their mums sat around spreading rumours about each other.

The grey sky threatened rain, but for the moment it was holding off. The boy wasn't concerned about that anyway. The others would rush away if a downpour broke out and he would have the entire park to himself, without anybody to disturb him. He didn't care if he got wet, and under the trees he would be protected from the rain just as he was protected from the attention of the other children and their parents.

The beetle was still crawling around the circular bottom of the jar while the boy walked stealthily through the trees, further away from the others. The destination was the ant castle.

He could still remember that Saturday at the garage sale, even though it was nearly a year ago. His mother had been better than usual at that time because she hadn't had a man in her life. The instant he'd seen the old toy castle, he'd known he wanted it, but it hadn't been until several months later that he envisioned its potential as an instrument of social research.

He considered the trapped beetle with curiosity. He suspected it wouldn't be able to integrate into the ant castle, but he needed to be sure of this assumption, and he had to know exactly how the ants would react to the presence of the outsider.

He slipped past the last tree before the ant castle. He was as far away from the football pitch as possible. On the far side of the ant castle, a rusty wrought-iron fence separated the park from a main road that was throbbing with peak-hour traffic. Headlights flickered through the bars of the park fence as drivers went through the usual evening routine of mindlessly accelerating and braking.

Gathering the ants had been more difficult than taking the beetle from its tree, but they had been easier to find. Once he'd located a nest, he'd placed the plastic castle next to it so the transfer would be as direct as possible.

He looked into the plastic castle. The ants were still inside. Some were trying to escape, but the moat which surrounded the fortified walls prevented the insect occupants from fleeing their stronghold.

He held the jar out over the castle and tipped it until the beetle fell onto the parade ground in front of the keep.

At first, nothing happened. But the boy was incredibly patient for his age.

He took a pen and notebook from his schoolbag so he could record his findings. Then he waited quietly, giving the castle his undivided attention.

He waited, motionless except for his writing hand. He noted every movement made by the beetle and the ants around it.

The voices of the other children faded away as they finished their football match and headed home for dinner. The grey sky continued to menace wet weather, but under the trees the boy was too occupied to worry about such a feeble distraction.

He continued waiting.

His stomach groaned with hunger, but that didn't matter. It could wait. His mother was probably still busy being beaten up anyway. He was better off waiting until the new boyfriend went out drinking, which would be at approximately seven o'clock if he followed his usual routine. The stupid man was even more predictable than the insects in the plastic castle.

Eventually, the ants started climbing over the beetle as though it were nothing more than a stone or a lump of soil. Then, realising what it was, they attacked.

It was like watching a miniscule army. They walked in line. One after the other, they came towards their prey and climbed onto it.

The boy smiled. It was just as he'd expected.

Dozens of tiny black soldiers worked their way over the protected body of the beetle. They were seeking the gaps between its plates of shell, just as a capable knight would have tried to thrust the blade of his broadsword between the plates of his adversary's armour. The ants identified their victim's weak points and concentrated their united strength.

A drop of water touched the boy's forehead, followed by others, but he paid little attention to this insignificant detail, just as he ignored the headlights flashing at him from the road. He was alone in his own world, hidden from view, observing from the outside without being observed himself. He was overlord of the ant castle.

The beetle, which had struggled pathetically at first, had since stopped moving altogether. It was no match for the disciplined ants, moving in unison in a way that human beings with their individual desires and difference of opinion would never be able to imitate. He thought about his mother. If only she had the ability to act more effectively. If only she could crush the beetle in her life. But she wasn't like an ant. She wasn't like a wolf either. She couldn't function socially and she was equally unable to survive alone. She needed him to look after her. A boy. But he wasn't yet capable of doing that. He was patient when it came to observing the beetle and ants, but his mother was a different story. He was less willing to sit back and watch her suffer. It wasn't right that she had to wait for him to grow up. She needed him to be a man for her now.

A drop of water fell on his brow and trickled down into an eye. This brought him out of his contemplation. It was time to go home.

He found a leafy branch and placed it gently over his castle, hiding it. Then he made his way out of the little wood and walked across the park, unconcerned by the cold rain soaking through his clothes and the wet grass licking his leather school shoes. As he trudged home, he hoped his mum's boyfriend would no longer be there when he arrived. It would be nice to enjoy a quiet evening without any hitting and screaming.

Once he'd reached the block of flats, he checked his letterbox, because he knew she sometimes forgot. But there was nothing. Most days they didn't receive any mail. There was the occasional bill or a letter from the bank, or a scribbled note from the boyfriend warning her that if she cheated on him, she would live just long enough to regret it. The nutcase wasn't worried about leaving tangible evidence of his violence in the letterbox because he knew she would never report him to the police. Women like her didn't do that. They accepted their status of victim. But unlike the ants with the beetle, her boyfriend didn't have to find gaps between plates of shell. Her body was soft and vulnerable all over.

He climbed the concrete stairs that led to the fourth floor balcony and a wave of relief washed over him. The new boyfriend wasn't there. He knew that before knocking on the door, because he heard no shouting or thumping, or those horrible rhythmic groans the pig of a man often made when he was having his way with her.

He knocked, and his mother answered the door immediately, melting when she saw it was him.

'There you are then,' she practically whispered. 'You know how I worry when you stay at the park until late.'

He didn't answer. He just looked at her, his face expressionless and rain-drenched. He was hoping the absurdity of her words would dawn on her, but she just smiled at him warmly, happy she was no longer alone. As he stepped inside and dropped his schoolbag on the floor without paying attention to where he was putting it, he surveyed the living room, confirming that his mother was alone.

'He won't be back for hours, honey.'

She bent over to kiss him on the cheek, exhibiting her battered body. Her arms bore several bruises of different sizes and colours, ranging from little purple ones to big yellow ones, and she had a swollen lip. These disfigurations were souvenirs from a beating she'd been dealt last week. He always looked at her arms and face when he arrived home to see if there were new signs of violence. Sometimes, in addition to her bruises and swollen lips, she had cigarette burns sadistically decorating her forearms. She didn't smoke much, but the pig was a chimney. Smokers, as far as the boy was concerned, were the dregs of humanity. The habit was a symbol of weakness, indiscipline, and filth.

Whenever she ventured into the street, she wore long sleeves to hide these monuments to her cruel relationship. What she'd thought was at long last a real love story had failed to ripen, instead rotting all the way to the core. Every bruise, burn, and scratch screamed this out loud. As for her face, she couldn't do much to cover up the bruises. She applied make-up and wore sunglasses, but above all, she stayed indoors as much as possible.

Not having much in the way of family or friends made the

masquerade easier, but she still had to find excuses to avoid meeting up with her precious few girlfriends.

She touched her son's wet head softly.

'You're soaking wet. Go and have a warm shower and put your pyjamas on.'

He did as he was told and his mother went back to preparing dinner for two while she watched Neighbours. Under the shower, he thought about his insect study. He expected to find the lifeless body of the black beetle the following afternoon. It would be exactly where he'd last seen it, and the ants would no longer be within the confines of the plastic castle. After having spent all that night and the following day working over the beetle, they would have found a passage out of the castle and back to their nest. He marvelled at the efficiency of little creatures while the warm water washed the cold out of his bones.

What did all that mean, about the ants and the beetle? He knew what the results would be, but he didn't really know why it was the case. How was the interaction to be explained? If only he could put his mother's new boyfriend into a plastic castle inhabited by hostile ants. Would the result be comparable? One could only hope so. That would be just ideal, to go to the park the following afternoon and find the lifeless corpse of that worthless excuse for a man lying over the plastic ant castle.

He laughed aloud as he washed behind his ears, just as mother always said he must.

'You nearly finished in there?'

'Yeah, mum!'

'The bangers are done.'

'All right. I'm coming.'

He washed his armpits.

Of course, ants couldn't possibly kill a man; not those belonging to any species found in Britain at any rate. Adjustments would be required. What would be the human equivalent of the beetle versus ant study? That was a difficult one to answer. Maybe he could conduct another kind of experiment on the new boyfriend. He looked over to the hand basin and medicine cabinet. The effects of hydrochloric acid in his aftershave lotion would be interesting, for example. The mental image of the brute having the lower half of his face burn away was immensely amusing.

He turned the water off, dried himself before stepping out of the shower enclosure, and put his pyjamas on. He was looking forward to a hot meal with mother; just the two of them. Hopefully, the new boyfriend wouldn't come back that night.

'How's everything going at school?'

'Fine, mum,' he replied dismissively as he sat himself at the table.

'That's good then.'

She gave him a generous serving of mashed potato. Schoolwork wasn't a problem. Precocious and perceptive were the words Mrs Thwaites had used the last time they'd met. She'd explained that gifted children require special attention, just as children with learning difficulties do. Both women were well aware that mother and school alike were ill-equipped to meet those needs.

'Did you see Simon's mum at the park today?'

'Yes,' he mumbled through the mashed potato in his mouth.

'What did she say? Did she ask you any questions about me?'

He shook his head and mixed another dollop of butter into his mash.

'She didn't speak to me, and I don't go near her. I have better things to do than talk to her.'

He cut up a sausage and stabbed a slice with his fork.

'If she asks anything, you just tell her I'm doing fine, but that I'm very busy at the moment.'

He grunted in agreement.

'All right?' she pressed.

'Sure, but I won't talk to her.'

The conversation stopped as they both concentrated on their food and the TV.

Ten minutes later, they'd both finished. The boy went to the living room and got stuck into his homework, which he usually completed in half the time it took his classmates. He was then free to read while his mum watched more soaps. The lives of the people in some of these shows were even more messed up than her own. This made her feel better, as though she wasn't the only woman with difficulties. Her son knew it also helped her complacently accept her lot in life.

They could stay together like that for hours, speaking very little but both happy to be together. She knew he liked to be with her and nobody else. He too understood that she liked to be with him. But precocious or not, he wasn't yet old enough to comprehend why she also felt the need to have the new boyfriend in her life despite all the pain he caused her. Maybe the day would come when he could fathom how a fully grown woman could choose to live with a man who did nothing but hurt her.

Not long before nine o'clock, she told him to stop reading and go to bed. He didn't argue. He didn't need to because he knew he would be able to continue reading without her knowing. He kept an old torch under the bed for that very purpose. She often wondered where his passion for reading came from. It certainly wasn't from her or his father. Perhaps it was some kind of genetic trait that had skipped a generation or two. Her maternal grandfather had been involved in some kind of complex project during the war, although she didn't know quite what since he'd always remained tight-lipped about those dark days.

'I love you, mum,' he said, knowing how much it meant to her, and hugged her.

'I love you, my little man,' she whispered. Her eyes were full of tender sadness. 'Go to bed now.'

He headed towards his room, but she called out.

'Don't forget to brush your teeth first.'

He altered his course and headed towards the bathroom.

'Acid in the toothpaste,' he said to himself as he brushed his teeth, spraying white spit over the mirror as he spoke. 'That would be even better than putting it in his aftershave.'

He frowned at his reflection. 'There's a problem with that idea. We all use the toothpaste. What if mum brushed her teeth before he did? I'll have to work on that one. I'd need to sort out the details to make sure she wasn't exposed to any risk.'

He gurgled and spat the toothpaste into the sink. He smiled at himself in the mirror, checking that his teeth were well brushed, before shuffling back to his bedroom and crawling under the blanket. He lay motionless, as though asleep, and remained like that for several minutes, until he heard the bedroom door creak open.

Mothers are so very predictable. He didn't like to manipulate her, but he had to read. He had to keep learning and growing as quickly as possible.

Once the door was closed again, he reached under his bed for the torch and flicked it on under the blanket. His mother wouldn't come to check on him a second time. He could read for as long as he liked now, until he felt too tired to stay awake.

Thirty pages later, he felt his eyelids being drawn down as though tugged at by the powerful and countless jaws of a troop of ant knights.

He slipped the bookmark into place and put the torch and book under his bed. He rested his head on his pillow and sleep quickly claimed him.

A noise disturbed him in the middle of night. He stared uselessly at the ceiling, hidden in the obscurity of the night.

The sound of a chair being jolted against the dining table broke through the silence.

There was no doubt about it. The pig was pissed and staggering through the flat, trying to find the bedroom where his female had been soundly sleeping before his arrival.

'We were sleeping, moron!'

He would have liked to shout it out, but he only dared mouth the words in hushed annoyance. He knew what would happen to him if he made the mistake of speaking up.

The slow, clumsy footsteps grew louder as the brute moved unsteadily towards her bedroom. He wanted to have his way with her before falling into a deep beer-induced slumber.

The boy heard the creaking hinges of her bedroom door, followed by a brief exchange. The words were quiet but violent. The boyfriend's voice grumbled drunkenly. Hers pleaded, telling him to go to sleep, but he started to grumble louder. She didn't want him to raise his voice because she knew it would wake her son. So, she let him do what he wanted.

A terrible silence reigned. They spoke no more. For a few long minutes, there wasn't a sound to be heard. Then the monster started to grunt. Disgusting. Rhythmic. It was like a pig trying to hum a tune.

It grew louder and louder.

She tried to hush him, but that made the grunting faster. She started to sob, but it was faint, as though filtered through her pillow. It sounded like a grotesque duet.

The boy didn't understand precisely why his mother was crying, but he was sick of it. She hadn't been crying before the pig's arrival.

'One day, I'll include you in one of my studies.'

He smiled to himself in the dark.

'That's right,' he nodded his head in agreement with himself. 'One day, you'll end up like the big black beetle.'

Previously Published

Cleopatra's Mystery Box, Nefariam: The Element of Crime, ID Press, 2020

The Church of Asag, SQ Mag #13, 2014

Old Mabel's Stray Cat, Fear, Crooked Cat Books, 2012

Veronica's Dogs, In Sunshine Bright and Darkness Deep, Australian Horror Writers Association, 2015

The Crows of Eildon Hill, Blue Crow Magazine #4, 2015

Lauren, Of Devils and Deviants, Crowded Quarantine Publications, 2014

Milk, The Literary Hatchet #13, 2015

Horror at Hollow Head, Lighthouses, Black Beacon Books, 2015

Forgotten Falls, Into the Woods, Hic Dragones, 2017

Animal, Monsters Amongst Us, Oscillate Wildly Press, 2016

Like Sisters, Morpheus Tales #31, 2017

It Starts with Insects, Dig Two Graves: Volume II, Death's Head Press, 2019

Entering the tunnels is easy, but Ripley and Gabriela soon discover that reaching the surface again will be the greatest challenge they have ever faced...

The Tunnel Runner is a tale of urban adventure and social discontent that plunges the reader deep beneath the city of Brisbane.

Come and explore the world on the other side of the street.

Also Available from Black Beacon Books

A short, stormy anthology designed to be read while the wind howls and the thunder booms. Batten down the hatches and take shelter!

For news, reviews, competitions, author interviews,
and exclusive excerpts

Visit our website
blackbeaconbooks.com

Follow us on Facebook
facebook.com/BlackBeaconBooks

Join us on X
@BlackBeacons

Subscribe on Patreon
patreon.com/blackbeaconbooks

www.blackbeaconbooks.com

www.ingramcontent.com/pod-product-compliance
Lightning Source LLC
Chambersburg PA
CBHW032140170626
46808CB00006B/2315